COMMITTED

2

DECEPTION

Coming soon by Nisha Le'Shea

Manhood

A Troubled Past

COMMITTED 2 DECEPTION

Nisha Le'Shea

nishalesheabooks@yahoo.com

For information about special discounts for bulk purchases, please email Nisha Le'Shea at nishalesheabooks@yahoo.com

Printed in the United States of America.
Book Cover Photograph by Michael Martin
Cover design by Nisha Le'Shea
Book edited by Santrell Davis

ISBN: 978-0-615-46908-9

To

A very special person, you know who you are :-)

I want you to know that I still and always will love you.

Thanks for always being a true friend.

And in loving memory of my aunt

MS VICKIE JEAN BROWN

(1955-2011)

The family misses you. Your memory and warm hearted

spirit will live in our hearts forever. I love you.

Acknowledgements

Only my Lord & Savior Jesus Christ had the power to pull me and the rest of my family through our lost. And, for that I want to thank him. I understand that you called your angel "Vickie" back home and I know that she's in a better place.

To my mother, in my eyes you truly are superwoman. Thanks for being my back bone, friend, and so much more. I can always count on you, no matter the circumstances.

To my best girl, TT Wells, author of, **Caught up in a Love Triangle**, all I have to say is, we are on our way to the top. We both will be self-made millionaires one day. Believe that! Never mind the critics.

To my best friend Joe Woolfolk Jr., I love you to death. You've always remained a true friend although at times, certain haters tried to make our friendship impossible. Thanks for being there for me during the times that I needed you the most. Love ya' always!!!

To my nephew Tyler, and little cousin Eva, you are truly an inspiration for me to push harder at succeeding in life. I want to be able to give you guys the world one day. To my nephew Amir, and, nieces Taylor and Chanel, auntie loves you soooooo much. To my oldest nephew Mikell, I love you dearly; keep up the good work in school. I'm proud of you. To my god daughter Ja'Lisha, continue making those straight A's and you already know anything that you want I'll make sure that you get it. To my god son Jalen, keep making me laugh. Silly boy! I love you.

To my uncle Eric thanks for all the encouraging words and support. Your success gives me motivation to give 100% at everything I do. You've taught me that people shouldn't only worry about today but what they can do today that will be beneficial for them in their future. All the talks we've had have played a major role in my decision making and helped me to become the hard-working woman that I am today. To my uncle Ramone, I look at you and I see the father that you are to your kids, the husband that you are to your wife, and I hope that my husband is just like you. Thanks for all the advice that you've given me over the years. Words cannot begin to express my appreciation.

To my aunts, Aunt Betty, and Lady "The Divas" I love ya'll. Aunt Betty thanks for never sugar coating anything and always telling people like it is, even though at times I didn't want to hear it. Basically I was just young and thought I knew it all, but as I got older I realized I didn't know everything, and learned to appreciate the lessons that you have always tried to teach not only me, but everyone. Lady, all that I have to say is when I make it to the top you will be right there with me. No doubt about it!

To my sisters Michaal and Melody, Ya'll chicks already know that when I make it to the top "Ya'll gon' be straight". To my two brothers Darrien and Mike, thanks for helping ma raise me (even though I'm the oldest) ya'll look out for me like I'm the little sister, I love ya'll. To my brother Miguel thanks for your sense of humor, you always know how to put a smile on my face.

To Treat, we've been friends since we were ten years old, and no matter what has been thrown our way we've always remained best friends. I Love you like a sister. To Brandon, man where shall I start! With your crazy ass! I'm just going to say this, thanks for always being there with a sympathetic ear when I need to vent. To Ashley, we've been best friends since we were eight years old and you've always treated me like family. Although we've lived in different cities for years and we don't talk every day, when we do talk it's like we never missed one day. That's the definition of true friendship. To Santrell, you were the first person to read this book and you told me that you believed in me and that I could do anything that I wanted to do as long as I worked hard at it, those words meant a lot to me and I want to thank you for all the encouraging words and everything that you've ever done for me. To Neka, thanks for bragging to all your friends about how great of a writer that I am, in your opinion, and pushing me to continue writing when I wanted to give up. You know, you and your mom are going to be straight to. Ya'll are like a second family to me.

To my cousins Valencia, Jamie, (the dance machines) I love ya'll. I look forward to family day on Sundays because I know that I'm sure to get a laugh watching the two of you party your butts off.

To my favorite cousin Kisha, I've enjoyed your company since you've been down here visiting. I'm going to miss you when you're back in New York.

Thanks for all the input you gave me while I was writing this book.

To Ms. Evelyn, I love you dearly you are like a second mom to me and I appreciate everything that you've ever done for me, and thanks for all the home cooked meals! LOL

To my Godmother Cynthia, you have always treated me like I was your birth daughter and nothing less, thanks for everything. I love you!

To Reggie Stubbs, thanks for purchasing my book before it was even finished. When you told me that you wanted to buy my book after you read the first chapter, even though that you knew I wasn't finished with it, made me come harder with every chapter thereafter. Thanks. To Val, you were always like a second mom to me. Thanks for all your moral support and helping hand when I needed you the most. To Teresa, we've only known each other for a short while, but you have made such a huge impact on my life. Keep raising those girls to grow up and be independent just like you. You're doing a good job! To Robert, thanks for all the spiritual quotes you tell me on the days that I'm at my worst. You truly are an angel in disguise!!!!

To Michael Martin, thanks for taking such a beautiful picture of my sister Michaal Jones. The book cover is hot!!!!

Thanks to everyone that has helped me along my journey, I don't know where I would be if I had not been blessed with your presence. I love you all from the tip of my soul and the bottom of my heart. Always remember that no matter what someone may do or say to try and discourage you from your dreams ignore them and keep working towards your goal because anything is possible as long as you have hard work, dedication, and determination.

COMMITTED 2 DECEPTION

1

ALEXIS

January 2011. Not a soul living could have told me that I would be in this predicament. How typical of me to think that I had it all figured out! Lately I've been through hell, and the face of the man that helped inflict bitterness upon me just appeared in my mind. I don't regret ending his life, hell, he deserved it. I'm the victim. I can't think of one good reason that I should have spared him his life. If you want to know the truth, I should have done it years ago.

What I really wish I could do is get back all those years I gave 'em, but life does not work that way. Most of our marriage I was bleak, and by the end of it, I turned to all types of medications to cope with the depression. They quit working some time ago, per my family and close friends; I'm on edge and crazy without them. Reality is, all those pills have done for me is zone me out, while my life has been stripped away from me inch by inch and piece by piece.

That explains why I'm lying here barely conscious: cold and trembling while sweat seems to somehow still be leaking through the pores of my body. I'm awaiting my death, which means that I've finally given up. Between the recent tragic experiences and constant betrayal, I've been beaten down. It's unbelievable that I've been able to last this long.

We got married so quickly, I hardly knew 'em. He turned out to be a pain in my ass for eight long years. Terrence was a womanizer; he preyed on every woman that became acquainted with him, with the help of his good looks and money. He was manipulative, and Pathological Liar should have been his birth name.

A good wife has a hot dinner ready when her husband gets home from work, she keeps the house clean, and at the end of the day she musters up the energy to be a freak between the sheets. I did all those things, and some! All I wanted was for him to respect me. Make better choices than he did. Sacrifice some of the ways that made him feel good, but hurt me. Simple but he couldn't do it. He continuously broke my heart over and over again. That's why I did what I did to 'em. Well, part of the reason I did it is because I've completely lost my mind. Surely I was outside of myself. Ever since the day we became married I've been stuck in his shadow, putting on a happy face for everyone around me. I've had it all money, cars, trips, and all the material things that a

2

woman would ever desire. But if I would have known then, what I now know, I would have given it all up for a shot of happiness.

Look at me: lying on the floor in my living room. My fingertips are cold, while nestled around the nearly empty bottle of Moscoto that I drank as I guzzled down the prescription bottle of Xanax pills that I had refilled earlier this week. I've reached rock bottom. *How could I let myself get to this point?* is the only thing that I'm thinking about at the moment.

Visually I'm beautiful. Well... normally I am, but not at the very moment. Right now I look like a damn Zombie, with rollers in my head, and I'm dressed in dingy loose fitted clothes. My skin is pale and I've lost at least twenty pounds between now and the last three weeks. If you didn't know me you would think that I'm a crack-head, because that's exactly what I look like today. Years ago you couldn't have paid me to carry myself the way I have been lately.

I'm weak and the room looks cloudy. My vision is becoming blurrier by the second. Hastily I'm losing consciousness, and the pace of my heart is slowing down. My mobile has rung back to back for the last twenty minutes. My weakness will not allow me to get my behind up off of this floor and retrieve it. So I ignore it, and close my eyes, hopefully for the last time.

The next thing I know: I'm being carried away in a stretcher, as I hear my mother crying frantically. "Alexis what have you done" after she emerges herself from the shock of my appearance she leaps into the ambulance truck. That question causes my emotions to be all over the place. I cringe at the mere thought of how I allowed myself to get to this point. Considering the fact that I was always taught that a man can only do to you what you allow. I was told to never say what your man will or will not do to you, and that way you'll never end up heartbroken. Those were the rules that I once lived by and for years I allowed no man the satisfaction of taking advantage of me. But that was long before I met the scum of the fucking earth.

With thirty six double D's a twenty five inch waist, forty inch hips, caramel colored smooth skin, and beautiful long black hair. I've always had men longing to be with me. I mean you name it! They all wanted to holler. I dated a couple of them but I never let things get to serious. That's why I never saw it coming. How was I supposed to know that I would soon become a fool in love and Committed 2 Deception? Hell, I never suspected it.

I can't help but wonder what my life would have been like if I had chosen not to seduce Terrence the day I laid eyes on him. I feel that my life would have been so much better if I had never met him. I'm thinking about my family and how they are going to question themselves on what has driven me to this point. But before they will ever understand how I got to this point, they must first understand how it all started. This is the story of my life.

2003. It almost felt like I was dreaming as I turned my head slightly; although I knew that I wasn't-because I was staring right at him as he entered the coffee shop. All six feet five inches of 'em. His dark smooth skin, pearl white teeth and bald head was enough to make any woman go head over hills for him. Not to mention he looked like he had a million dollars in his bank account. After about five minutes of going back and forth in my mind about whether or not I should approach him, I decided against it. Instead I pranced past him strutting what my mama blessed me with, heading to the ladies room, knowing that he would notice my sweat pants hugging my ass, revealing my famous apple bottom.

Once I was in the ladies room I fiddled around a little, after I was done glossing my luscious lips and making sure that everything on my one hundred thirty five pound frame was perfect.

Back at the table I was reading the daily paper as I sipped on a cup of hot tea. While sitting alone I longed for his attention and I wanted badly for him to become the man in my life. I never thought that from that day forward my life would be changed forever. Not necessarily for the best.

"Mind if I join you?" He asked rhetorically as he stood in front of me.

"Not at all" I responded trying not to seem desperate.

"My name is Terrence Johnson" he said. "What's yours?"

He pulled the empty chair from underneath the table and sat down.

"Alexis Williams" I answered.

"I don't see a ring on your finger. So I take it that you don't have a man?" He questioned, scooting the chair closer to the table using his feet.

"Just because I don't have a ring on my finger doesn't mean that I don't have a man" I struck back.

"Well it must not be too serious because if you were my woman you'd definitely have a ring on your finger" He took off his jacket and placed it across the top of the chair.

"What makes you so sure of that?" I asked flirtatiously.

"Go on one date with me and you'll find out"
He gave me a cocky look as if he could see right through me. As if he knew exactly what I'd been contemplating ever since I saw him walk through the door.

"Well aren't we confident" I joked. "But I'm curious to know what makes you say that I'd have a ring on my finger if I were you woman, being that you don't know anything about me"

"I'm not worried about that because pretty soon I'm sure that I'll know everything about you"

"Are you sure about that?" I asked trying not to give into his arrogance.

"Just to prove to you how sure I am" He leaned forward and grabbed his wallet from his back pocket and handed me an undisclosed amount of cash. "Go out and buy yourself something nice to wear out on our date tonight."

"I haven't said that I'm going to go, for all you know I could just take this money and do whatever I want to do with it." Without counting the money I stuffed it in my bra.

"You're right, you could do that, but I know that you won't"

Blah Blah Blah….We shared the usual conversation before he stood. "I'll pick you up around seven thirty at the student hall"

My heart skipped a beat. My mouth and eyes were opened wide as I inquired in a frightened tone. "How do you know that I live in the dorms?"

"Don't worry I'm not a stalker. I see you down the street sometimes getting your wig shook. Your beautician Lisa and I are close friends and she's told me all about you" He explained with a charming smile. "Be ready at seven thirty" He ordered. He collected his coat, finished up the last swallow of his coffee, and walked away.

"I never said that I was going" I pressed.

"You'll be ready" He turned to me and said before exiting the door.

It killed me to know that Lisa hadn't told me anything about Terrence…I mean she was my best friend. She knew me like the back of her hand, so I was pretty sure that she knew that Terrence was the type of guy I'd been searching for. We'd been best friends since our senior year in high school and back then we were like the thickest thieves. You would never see one of us, without seeing the other. However by now, we almost never spent any time together. She'd married a local drug king in Atlanta that went by the name of King Pen. People treated him like God. He'd purchased Lisa her own hair salon and the shit was laid. They lived in this grand seven hundred thousand dollar house. They both pushed foreign cars well over 80k a piece. Most of her time was spent with him, whenever he wasn't out of town on business. For me, I was never fond of him. There was something sneaky about him, that I could never quite put my finger on.

My first impression of Terrence was that he was a very prestigious man. Judging from the corvette that I watched him get into, in the parking lot of the coffee shop, I knew that he was a well-paid brother. He definitely wasn't broke. He looked debonair that day dressed in a button down collared shirt, slacks, and a pair of shoes designed by Prada. The brother had it going on. The way he smelled had me all wet and bothered, and I would have done anything to be his lady.

During that time my transportation was a nineteen eighty nine Honda Civic and I was a sophomore at Spellman without a clue what I wanted to do with my life. My dream was to pursue my passion for singing and dancing. Once I graduated high school I had hopes of moving to New York and becoming a superstar. But my mother insisted that I attend a college close to home and major in a field that guaranteed stability. In her eyes singing and dancing has never been a reliable source of income. Her favorite thing to say was "you don't want to be like me, a mother of seven by the age of twenty three, and a janitor." I admired my mother and I wouldn't be able to live with myself if I disappointed her. That is why I never moved out of the state of GA. Trying to satisfy her, I put my dreams on hold, and part of me felt like I owed her that much. She'd sacrificed a lot for me and my other siblings, working two jobs and sometimes three to support us.

My daddy was quite the opposite. He was a jealous drunk that couldn't keep a job to save his life. In his younger days, he use to beat my mother every night, not seeming to care that his small children was in the next room hearing every blow that he gave her and every cry that she hollered. I can remember asking myself as a little girl, why does my mama put up with daddy? Why can't she just take us and leave in the middle of the night like Tina did in What's Love Got to Do with It? But she never did. He'd always make up a boggiest excuse for his behavior, and just like that, she would let him back into our lives. Then she would make up excuses for him when our family members would ask what on earth possessed her to take him back again. Those situations alone were the not the best example of how a man should treat a woman, or how a woman should let a man treat her. Somehow despite my childhood, I did my best to protect my heart from any man that reflected my father.

It was two months later and things couldn't be better. Ever since I was a little girl I dreamed about the type of man that I would marry. Terrence matched the description.

Family oriented, fine, wealthy, respectful, oh and did I mention fine. I think I did. If Terrence could have been arrested for his good looks he would be sentenced to life without parole. I once believed that I was the luckiest woman in the world. I had all his sexiness to myself. That man made me feel like I won the lottery and he was my winning ticket. Whining, dining, and showering me with all the finer things. It almost felt like it was too good to be true. And the sex: Oh my goodness! It was off the Richter scale. I was a little hot in the tail- as my mama would say- back in my younger days, I'd been having sex for about seven years by then, and had never known the pleasure of having an orgasm until I began screwing around with Terrence. All I thought about was having steaming hot sex with 'em. I craved for it all the time. His touch, his voice, his lips, and there wasn't anything that I wanted more than to share a life with him. Most people thought that what I was feeling was only infatuation, giving the short time that we'd known each other, but hell, I loved 'em. And I was falling for him more and more every day.

The only problem was that he was already taken. I only found that out a week before our two months anniversary. I'm not going to lie; it threw me for a loop when I answered my phone thinking that it was Terrence, but ended up having a heated argument with his wife, and learned that they'd been married for ten years.

"Hey baby" I said answering my cellular.

"This is not Terrence bitch. This is his wife, the woman that he's been married to for ten years now" She snapped.

"His wife?" I stuttered stunned by what she'd said.

"I didn't stutter bitch you heard me correct. You bitches are all the same, always claiming that you don't know that he's married. Let me ask you a question. What do you think that he's going to do…leave me?" Listen bitch start screwing your own man and leave my man the hell alone."

"First of all Terrence didn't tell me that he's married. Second of all, let me ask you a question. How does my pussy taste? Huh? I don't here you saying anything. Your husband has been eating my pussy for the last month" I chuckled.

I could hear her vomiting through the phone before we were disconnected. I guess the thought of her husband eating another woman's pussy and then coming home to her must have made her sick to her stomach. Back then I could care less about another woman's feelings. Her words did stick to me though. Suddenly all the pieces started to come together. That's why we would always have to meet up at the office, or on the other side of town. More than likely it was the reason why it had been two months since we'd been dating, and he'd never invited me to his home. Not even once. After reality kicked in, my laughs turned into tears. Who was I kidding? I felt like a fool. I was nothing more than a chick on the side, and there I was thinking that I was his one and only. His wife had the access to the bank account-the keys to the house-the stability. All I had was some great sex and a hot pack of lies. She had what I wanted and I wasn't going to rest until he was all mines. Of course I confronted him about the whole ordeal. His truth was that they were married, but he was not happy and eventually he was going to divorce her. Most women would say that I was a fool for believing him, but those are the women that have never- and probably will never meet a guy with the qualities that I saw in Terrence. I was so caught up in his lavish lifestyle, that I didn't give a damn what people had to say any how! I figured, why would I go back to rags, when I'd been blessed with riches? And that's how I ended up in this situation.

Have you ever heard the saying, how you get a man is the same way that you will lose him? In 2004 Terrence's ex-wife had-had enough of his lies and deceit and ended up leaving him. As he'd promised, the two of us became husband and wife, in the same year that his divorced was finalized. Yes! I was a fool and married his trifling ass. Being as though Terrence was a doctor and could afford anything, we had the most beautiful and elegant wedding any woman could dream of. In the beginning marriage was great, and I felt that Terrence couldn't do anything wrong. That was my first mistake. No. I take that back, my first mistake was marrying his ass in the first place. This makes me putting up with all his infidelity my second mistake. Ever since I'd been old enough to date I'd never been the woman to put up with bullshit. For

12

some reason things were different with him. I put up with more women claiming that they'd been intimate with my husband than he had patients, and he was a damn gynecologist. Now I had the answer to those questions that I asked myself as a child. Finally I realized why my mama put up with my daddy for all those years, and, all that I could say was never say, never. The only difference between my dad and Terrence was their bank accounts.

There are several reasons why I didn't want to leave Terrence, but the main reason was because he was one of the wealthiest men in Atlanta. Now don't try and judge me because you wouldn't have left him either, especially when his bank account statement showed seven figures. Hell pussy is valuable, no matter what we say to try and deny it; we never truly give it up for free. Even if the men we're giving it up to can only cut the grass, or repair the leak under the sink. After we give 'em some, we think they owe us something. Any woman that claims to differ is the same woman that's lying up with a man that can't do shit for her, fucking her for free.

I'd graduated from college, and I left home every day headed to a job that I hated. But hey, I didn't complain. Terrence paid off all the debt I accumulated in college, and paid for my tuition during my junior and senior year. He was the source for my position as a pharmaceutical manager, because he was friends with the district manager. In my eyes he'd paid the cost to be the boss over my life. And I followed his every command.

2

ALEXIS

3 years had passed and I'd begun to hate my marriage. Hate is a powerful word, to use to define a marriage. However I tried my best to bury my true feelings inside. It had gotten to the point where I couldn't remember the last time that I felt happy or even smiled. I was being neglected in the home that I shared with my husband. Our marriage was starting to feel more like an obligation rather than a desire to be with one another.

Vividly I remember, sampling the steak, before I placed our plates on the table. Then I went upstairs to start the water in the Jacuzzi. I poured two glasses of wine to go along with our meal. What was the special occasion? November 12, 2007 marked our third year anniversary. As soon as Terrence walked through the door it was going to be time to get down to business. Business meaning: screw; make love, fuck or whatever you want to call it. I was in need of a long overdue orgasm. I'd lost track of the last time I had one. I'd been horny ever since I stepped out of the bed that morning. Honestly speaking I'd been feening for it since the last time we did it. Terrence had been so busy with work, that by the time he made it home I was already asleep, or he was too tired to do it.

I made sure that I was looking good, flaunting my silhouette by wearing a red sheer gown that I purchased from Victoria's Secret a few months back when Lisa and I were at the Lennox Mall. I wore Brittany Spears Fantasy, Terrence's favorite perfume. Need I say that I was looking sexy as hell! So after I made sure that everything was perfected, I awaited my husband's arrival in the living room. *There is no way that he's going to say that he's too tired tonight* was the thought that lingered in my mind as I sat there on the love seat with my leg thrown across the arm of it, wearing no panties (might I add).

I took a sip of wine and sung along softly to Luther Vandross if only for one night. Right after I hung up the phone once I heard the recording to Terrence's voicemail for the sixth time. Or maybe it was the tenth. Hell I couldn't keep count. All I knew was the food had gotten cold and the candles had burned out. And there was still no sign of Terrence. Was I pissed off? Hell yeah! For four hours I paced back and forth from the living room to the kitchen wondering aloud where in the hell was Terrence.

I envisioned that we'd be done making love by then, and we'd be lying in bed as our naked bodies tempted each other to go for round two, or we'd either be feeding one another the chocolate covered strawberries that I had made earlier that day. Instead I was sitting there alone- calling his cell, his best friend, his job, hell I don't even know why I even bothered calling his job.

After I was placed on hold for nearly twenty minutes before his assistant came back to the phone only to say "Sorry Mrs. Johnson I can't seem to reach Dr. Johnson but as soon as I can get a hold of him, I'll tell him that it's urgent that he calls home." only confirmed that I shouldn't bother calling there. I was never the least bit convinced that she didn't know if whether or not he was there. Hell in my mind she may have been screwing 'em.

Lisa calling me at twenty minutes after ten the next morning is what awoke me. At that time I realized that I'd fallen asleep on the chase in our living room and also that Terrence never made it home. I picked up the phone talking sleepily while yawning.

"I'm not going to be able to make it this morning"

"Do you want to reschedule for next Saturday? sounds like somebody had a hellofva' night." She joked.

I ignored her statement and replied. "Next Saturday is good for me. I'll talk to you later girl." Assuring her that it wasn't a good time for small talk.

"Okay. Well you get some rest and call me later."

16

We both hung up the phone and before I could put the receiver back on the base, the sound of Terrence's footsteps echoed in my ear. I noticed that he was still dressed in his clothes from the day before as he sprinted pass the living room.

"Where in the hell have you been all night" I asked with a voice full of agony startling Terrence and stopping him dead in his tracks."

"I was at the hospital, two of my patients went into labor last night" He uttered in a low tone, still standing in the foyer.

"I called your phone numerous times last night. And you didn't answer any of my calls. The least you could have done was answer the damn phone and let me know that you were okay." I said with much attitude walking from the living room into the foyer.

"Look Alexis, my battery was dead okay. I've been up all night, and the only thing that I want to do is take a quick shower and go to bed." He was now walking towards the stairs.

While following in his tracks I asked. "What is more important to you…your career or our marriage?"

He turned to me before he stepped foot onto the step and stared at me with disappointment as if he couldn't believe that I'd asked him that question. "What kind of question is that?" He asked.

With tears in my eyes I argued "A man that cares about his marriage would have called his wife on their anniversary. He wouldn't have stayed out all night leaving her all alone."

Terrance gazed into my eyes and pleaded. "Baby I'm sorry that you are upset. Yes. I do love my career but nothing is more important to me than you and you should know that"

"I don't feel like I'm the most important person in your life because--

That's when his whole demeanor changed. Instantly he became irate as he cut me off in midsentence. "Alexis we can talk about this later. I'm too tired to talk about this right now. You live in this seven hundred thousand dollar house-which you don't have to worry *about* putting a dime on when the mortgage is due. All those luxury cars in the garage I pay for. Oh! And that rock on your finger, it wasn't cheap either. And I don't want to begin talking about how expensive your education was. So I don't want to hear any of your bitching and complaining today" He said as he walked up the steps.

By now we'd made it into our bedroom and Terrence had grabbed himself a pair of undergarments out of the armoire.

"You never want to hear what I have to say" I shouted standing directly behind him attempting to follow him into the bathroom. He slammed the door before me. Overwhelmed with frustration I pounded on the door with all the energy I had in me. Fed up with his inconsiderate actions towards my feelings I screamed. "WORK-WORK-WORK that's all you care about. When are you ever going to have time for me?" I wanted so badly to

18

kick down the door and force him to listen to me. But it wouldn't have served a purpose. Once I heard the water running in the shower, I figured why waste the energy. Clearly my feelings were not of his concern.

I went into the walk-in closet and changed into one of my fitted rompers. Slid on a pair of my Chanel pumps, grabbed the keys to the Rover and made my way back downstairs. I slammed the door as hard as I could when I stormed out. With all the tension between Terrence and me, I needed some me time.

3

TERRENCE

I shouldn't be surprised by the way Alexis stormed out in such a convulsive matter, she has every reason to be upset with me, and I had every reason to convince her stay. But guilt wouldn't allow me to do so. As I lather up the wash cloth with soap, the hot water pounding up against my flesh is releasing the tension in my muscles. If only a shower could wash away infidelity. I'm trying my best to forget about last night, but my mind can't escape my thoughts. The flashbacks are coming back to back like contractions. And my actions can't be erased. I'm musing over the fact that only an hour ago I awoke to a beautiful half naked women other than my wife lying next to me. Wow, what a hell of a night! It definitely did not turn out the way that I anticipated. My motive was to boast myself inside my wife, after savoring every drop of her sweet juices until she begged for me to stop. But instead I ended up becoming very acquainted with a drop dead gorgeous and very sexy co-worker. Ever since I laid eyes on Nicole in the break-room I found myself undressing her with my eyes every time that I saw her. The more I tried to elude temptation the more my emotions and physical desires kept getting the best of me. So I jumped at the first opportunity to get between her legs. Now that I'm sober and reality sets in, I wish that I can take it all back. If only I had thought about the consequences before I spent the entire night in another's woman's bed on me and my wife's anniversary.

As I step foot out of the shower my head feels like it's going to explode. I'm hung over and completely agitated with myself for my incautious behavior. Seldom do I spend the entire night with other women but the shots of liquor that I indulged at a sports bar after work yesterday only induced my conniving behavior.

With the towel wrapped around my waist, I'm standing in front of the sink, peering at the man in the mirror. With only one question in mind: what was I thinking going up in ol' girl bare? Being intoxicated and caught up in the moment damn sho' isn't any excuse. I'm a doctor. I know the statistics of HIV. How could I have been so stupid and risk jeopardizing the health of my marriage? Don't get me wrong that wasn't the first and it definitely won't be the last time that I cheat on my wife but I always use protection. I slip up every now and then but that's only once I've gotten to know a woman and she's proved to me that she isn't running all over Atlanta fucking every Tom, Dick, and Jerry. Not trying to call Nicole out of her name or anything but she definitely gave it up way to easy. Which only proves to me, that I'm not the only man she's hopped into bed with; so easily. Seems to me that-that's how she communicates, thinking that her pussy will give her rights to a man. Please! Not this man. It wasn't that I couldn't see through her coke bottle figure and mesmerizing smile last night, it's just after I started to feel buzzed I only had one goal in mind. And that was getting my dick wet between her thighs. Besides, like I said, ever since I laid eyes on her my desires have been getting the best of me. What was supposed to be a couple of hours of small talk amongst co-workers escalated into something so much more, and it could have all been avoided if I had chosen to be the devoted husband that my wife deserves.

While shaking my head, I let out a long sigh before I turned on the water and begin splashing it onto my face. I brush my teeth, put on my boxer briefs and walk slowly into my bedroom. I'm lying across the foot of the bed and here comes the flashbacks again……..

Late yesterday evening. After about an hour of conversation and a few drinks, the four other people that accompanied Nicole and I, all started to leave one by one, leaving me and Nicole the only two people sitting at the table.

"Come and dance with me" She said pulling me to the dance floor.

She had a seductive look in her eye like she was contemplating something so much more than a dance. Thinking with the head in my pants I didn't hesitate to follow behind her, zoned out from the alcohol, knowing that I was about to be in deep shit. We embraced, grinded, laughed, and just had a good time. To others it may have seemed that we were a pair. But little did they know, Nicole was single, and I had someone waiting on me at home. Unfortunately, at the time, neither of us cared. At least I know I didn't. I was too busy enjoying Nicole's perky breast rubbing against my chest and plumped ass in the palm of my hand. The temptation was becoming all too intense and I would be lying if I were to say that I was worried about my wife.

"Will you come home with me tonight?" Nicole asked me seductively.

"You know that I can't do that" I told her knowing that I was lying through my teeth.

"Why not? You might as well. You know that you want the same thing that I want"

"And what's that?" I continued sarcastically.

"Quit acting like you don't know what I'm talking about."

"You know that I'm a married man!"

"And? Are you trying to tell me that you've never stepped out on your wife before?"

"I'm not saying that, but I will say that I've never been intimate with a co-worker. I never mix business with pleasure. It's a recipe for disaster."

"Well it's a first time for everything. Look let's not play games okay. Why don't we just go back to my place and relish in each other's body? I understand that you're married, trust, I don't want anything more than one night of passionate love."

In my mind, I was thinking *what does she mean?* Passionate love my ass! I only want to seduce you, sex you, and swing on to the next one. Don't get it twisted. I fuck other women; I make love to my wife. There is a difference. But like most men I ignored all the indications that I might be dealing with a woman that will somehow confuse sex with love. The temptation was a motherfucker and the next thing I knew, I was barreling through the front door of Nicole's condo, wasting no time following behind her as she guided us into her bedroom. She slid off her clothes, pulled her shoulder length hair into a ponytail, and didn't give me time to do anything before she yanked down my pants and pulled the head of my penis out my boxer briefs. The moans were uncontrollable as Nicole salivated all over my dick, better than any woman has ever done before. The warmth from her mouth was feeling all too good and I was enjoying every second of it. About a minute into it, I felt myself about to burst. So I tried to preclude myself from exploding by forcing her away from me. Hungry for me she got off of her knees and stood before she sat down on my lap and nudged all nine inches of my bare manhood inside of her, riding it like she'd been craving for it all day. My hands caressed her soft breast, as my tongue suckled her hardened nipples. The expressions on her face were ones of pleasure and pain. But more pleasure than pain. She groaned my name as she moved my hands onto the areas of her body that she longed for me to touch. Her eyes were closed shut as she mumbled to me that she was cumming, with one hand on my chest and the other massaging her clit. We both ignored my iPhone, which had gone off for the fifth time in two minutes. By now her legs had started trembling and she was almost near her peak. Her pussy muscles were clinching; squeezing my dick tightly and the feeling was driving me wild. I attempted to boost her off of me but I couldn't contain myself in time. I burst inside of her. She jumped up afterwards, but there was no need. The damage had already been done.

I started a shower afterwards, and hoped she didn't ask to join. She didn't. Thank God. The chase was over, and I no longer wanted to be with her in that way. It wasn't until after it was over that I started to think about Alexis and how unimportant she must've been feeling. I wanted to go home to her, hold her, but my conscious was eating me up. So what did I do? I made the selfish decision to stay the night. Several hours later I recalled myself lying in dismay, with a woman that was pretty much a stranger. I was thinking about how I'd contrived in something that could cost me everything and I was very upset with the choice that I'd made. I didn't even remember her last name. All I knew was. She had a big ass and a cute face. But that wasn't enough for me to hurt my wife. For the last two months I wanted to give it to her with every inch that I had. Then, only twenty minutes after fucking her brains out, I wished that I could take it all back.

This morning I awoke to an excruciating headache, heavy eyes and a worse conscious than yesterday. Once I coasted Nicole over a little, because she was lying so close to me, it was impossible for me to sneak out of the bed without waking her, I grabbed my car keys, and forced my shoes on before I walked out of the door. Not even saying goodbye. Next, I started the engine of my vehicle and fled to the other side of town while I rehearsed the many lies that I was going to tell my wife, about my whereabouts. All kinds of emotions were traveling through my body and questions as well. The question that stuck out to me the most was whether or not Nicole was lying to me when she told me that she was on the pill. My head was and still is, all over the place.

Finally I made it home, unlocked the door, pushed it open and made my way into the house. Alexis wasted no time stopping me before I went up the steps. I didn't think she would be up so early. I assumed that I would have time to get myself together before having any type of interaction with her. So of course I told her the lie that I'd rehearsed in the car. That I'd been working all night. That was the only logical excuse that I could come up with for staying out all night. Whether she bought it I really can't say, but I sure as hell couldn't bring myself to

26

tell her truth. We argued. She stormed out. And now I'm the one doing all the calling. I know she's just sitting there screening my calls. But it's cool; because all I have to do is take her on the guilt trip ride. Make her feel like everything is her fault. Then she'll start blaming herself. I'll forgive her, and everything will be back to normal. It always works.

I only have a few hours to rest, before I'm scheduled for surgery. Ever since Dr. O'Neal had a stroke I've had to practice not only with my patients, but his as well. Boy is it taking a toll on my body. However work is going to be awkward today because I have to face Nicole. And all I can say is, Damn! Because I know that I've fucked up.

4

ALEXIS

I hopped into my SUV and sped off like a bat out of hell. By me not having anywhere to go, I was cruising around the city.   For the month to be November, the weather was perfect sunny with a cool breeze blowing through the air; it reminded me of the trips that Terrence and I had taken to South Beach. There were kids out playing, couples holding hands, families barbecuing. Everyone appeared to be happy and content with where they were in their lives. That was the life I longed for. I mean sure enough I had the Range Rover for the road trips- the Corvette whenever I was tired of driving the Rover- the Benz for work- the house with more than enough room for two people- the jewelry, and the man with seven figures. On the outside looking in you would think that my life was all peaches and cream. Well let me-let you in, on a little secret. My life was no fairytale. All I had were material things, and none of those things could ever substitute for L.O.V.E.

The more that I thought about it I realized that I was being controlled by the root of all evil, money. I cried, uncontrollably trying my best to hide the tears behind my Chanel sunglasses. I grabbed a tissue out of the glove compartment and damped it gently across my Mac perfected face, because the tears were uncontainable. I'd allowed Terrence to shower me with money, vehicles, vacations, and so on-for so long that he knew that if he bought me a bracelet or a new car, it would shut me up and excuse him from all the bullshit that he was putting me through. The sad thing was the little scenario had worked for three years. Hell he'd been doing it for so long that it was too late to try and change him.

Dangerously in love was the ringtone that was assigned to Terrence's mobile number. Every time I heard those words coming from my mobile I would smile. No matter how pissed off I was with him, my whole mindset would change. I'd be happy again. Ain't that crazy? And that particular day I loved every second that I was away from the house, beause he was blowing my phone up. Answer this question for me... How is it that, a man, an ignorant man at that has the power to alter a woman's mood? In my case it was my husband. Why? Why did I give 'em so much power? When Terrence and I were good, it was like I was in heaven. And when we were on bad turns, I was a bitch that was mad with the world.

It was three hours since I'd left the house in a frenzy, and I'd ignored all fifty million of Terrence's calls. I called myself trying to give him a dose of his own medicine. I knew exactly what I was doing. He hated it when I didn't answer when he called. So I knew that he was going to be upset. And frankly I didn't give a damn.

When I walked into the house he was sitting in the living room with the remote in his hand flipping through the television and eating a bag of potato chips. I looked at the expression on his face and I knew that he was displeased with me "Terrence" I said. He didn't answer. So I stood directly in front of the television.

"I know you hear me talking to you Terrence"

"And I know you heard your phone ringing. Now move, I'm trying to watch the game" He said.

"We need to talk" I told 'em as I turned off the television that hung over the fireplace.

"Oh, now you want to talk! Why in the hell you weren't answering when I was trying to call you?" Using the remote he turned the T.V. back on.

"I didn't hear it ringing" I lied with a straight face.

"Yeh right" He put the remote down on the coffee table and walked into the kitchen.

I followed behind him, furious out of my mind. He'd grabbed a bottle of water out of the fridge and was twisting off the cap.

"So let me get this right! Your excuse to the reason why you didn't answer your phone last night is excusable, but mine isn't?"

I was standing with my hands on my hips and becoming irate by the seconds as I watched the man I love more than my own life ignore my question and chase down the chips with the water as if he hadn't heard a word that I said. I saw that my tactics weren't working so I changed the subject.

"Well what did you want? What was your reason for calling me?"

"If you hadn't been acting so damn childish, and answered your phone, you wouldn't be asking me that question. Now would you? Where are your car keys?"

"Why?"

"Because I'm taking your car"

"They're in living room on the mantle. And, where are you going?"

"Last time I checked I was a grown ass man, and I don't have to explain my every move to you, But I have to be back to work at a quarter to three, if you must know." He walked back into the living room and grabbed the keys off the mantle.

"Why do you have to take my car" I asked trailing in his tracks.

"Because I pay the note, that's why."
He walked out of the room, and in no time he'd left the house. I watched him drive off. Then I nodded my head in disbelief, because once again, like always he'd turned his inconsiderate behavior around on me as if he was the victim.

"*Work my ass. He always flips shit around on me and does his best to manipulate me into being the bad person. He gets on my damn nerves thinking that shit always has to go his way.*" I said loudly stumping across the hardwood floors. I made my way into our bedroom and became even more upset as I rounded up the rose pedals and what was left of the candles, which were supposed to help me seduce a night of heated sex and foreplay. I took a deep breath and sat down on the bed. The sheets were still in place, only wrinkled at the bottom. The pillows were cold and the anniversary card that I positioned on the pillow of Terrence's side of the bed was untouched. He didn't even attempt to read it.

It had been hours since Terrence left and I was beginning to blame myself for our little dispute. I tried to call 'em and apologize. As usual I was sent to the voicemail. The loneliness was becoming too familiar. And the only way that I knew how to make things right was to point the finger towards myself for our many problems: which led to me reminiscing about all the nights that Terrence and I made hot passionate love.

The one time that I remember so vividly is when Terrence and I took a seven day trip to Denver Colorado. Next to graduating from college, it was the happiest day of my life. The snow was pulsating against the window and the heat from the burning fireplace had the cabin nice and cozy. We were drinking hot cocoa and playing scrabble. I was winning the game, but when I came back

32

from tinkling Terrence had cleared the game board, leaving only a few letters on it. Pouting because I was under the assumption that he was trying to cheat, that I didn't realize what the letters read. But as I examined the board more closely, I recognized what he'd spelled out. I turned around with the happiest expression on my face and there he was down on one knee, with a seven caret princess cut diamond ring.

"Do you want to have a big happy family, with a big house and acres of land for the kids to run around on?" He asked nervously.

"Yes" I answered anxious for him to pop the big question.

"I can give you all of that plus a life full of love, joy, and happiness, if you promise to grow old with me"

"Yes! Baby Yes" I shouted kneeling down to kiss 'em. I paused and backed away from him "Wait minute is the divorce final yet?"

"It was finalized last week and I can't wait until the day that you become Mrs. Johnson" He stated before he carried me to the king sized bed. Within two minutes he'd stripped me naked and was massaging my kitty with his tongue. The blissful caress of his tongue sucking, nibbling and kissing every inch of my secrets was all too powerful. I belonged to him and he belonged to me in that moment. I climaxed before he entered inside of me. Right when I thought it couldn't get any better he flipped me over on all fours and stroked slowly causing me to fall deeper in love with him-with every stroke.

With this vision in my mind I erased our previous argument from my head. And once Terrance came back home-which was several hours later I accompanied him in the shower. After I bathed him and made sure that his manhood was clean I sucked him until my jaws became sore. I was hungry for him. He nourished my hunger pangs, with every moan, and every groan that he uttered. I was in control and getting full through his emotions. Immediately after the oral sex we made magic on the sink in the bathroom, my legs were wrapped around his waist, my fingers were scratching his masculine back while he whispered in my ear.

"Oh baby it's so good and tight. This pussy is mines forever. You better not give it to anybody else"

"It's yours" I moaned back.

My eyes rolled to the back of my head. I was almost at that place-the place I would go when we made love. His strokes were starting to get shorter, quicker and more aggressive. A few seconds later he released his tension as he jerked, and grunted inside of me. My legs quaked as I lost control of myself. I was finally having that long overdue orgasm. And boy was it long overdue!

Afterwards I was sore from trying to hold my balance up on the sink. I asked him for a massage but he said that he was too tired. He rolled over to his side of the bed. I pulled in closer to him and wrapped my leg around his. Our naked bodies touched, and yet it still felt like we were miles and miles apart. I was silent and staring at the ceiling, for a short while before I gathered the nerve to tell 'em that we needed to talk.

"Can we talk?" I asked reluctantly.

"Can this wait?" He insisted, sounding as though he was aggravated.

"No. Not really"

"And why is that?" He questioned me flipping over his pillow.

It pissed me off when he would do that; answer my question with a question, because my questions would never get answered. Why couldn't he see that our marriage was in shambles?

"Terrence we're having marital problems, and I need to know why you have been so distant lately. I don't feel like-------." I paused and let out a long sigh.

"I'm listening" He mumbled as if what I was saying to him was going to go in one ear and out of the other.

"I don't feel like we have the connection that we had when we first got married. We hardly do anything fun anymore. We never talk. You're so busy with work that you never have time for me. I just want to put the romance back into our marriage. I love you too much to let our marriage go down the drain."

I paused again our bedroom was quiet as I waited for a response. He didn't say anything. "Terrence is you listening to me?" He still did not respond. I used my knee in an effort to get his attention. I heard him snoring. He'd fallen asleep. *"What kinda' husband would go to sleep on his wife in the middle of her crying her heart out to 'em?"* I quoted. I snatched away the comforter from him. Wrapped it around my sore body and cried myself to sleep.

5

ALEXIS

"Good morning Lexi Pooh" Terrence said as I strolled into the kitchen that following morning.

"Good morning" I mumbled barely loud enough for him to hear it. He handed me a plate of pancakes, with sausage, and scrambled cheese eggs. That he'd whipped up. He tried to plant a kiss on my forehead but I turned away from him and walked over to the breakfast bar. I put my plate down and walked over to the refrigerator.

"You can't tell your husband good morning"

"I said good morning" I snapped back, bending down to get the syrup out of the refrigerator.

"What's wrong with you?"

"It doesn't matter, you don't care anyway." I was now walking back to the table.

"It's not like I can read your mind" He came up behind me and wrapped his arms around my waist.

"I'm sorry babe. Look I know that things haven't been going so well between us lately-and I know that I'm the blame for most of our marital problems. But I promise that I'm going to make it up to you."

He gave me a succulent kiss on the neck before he pulled the chair out for me. I sat down and began eating. He grabbed his glass off of the table drunk the last sip of his orange juice and put the empty glass in the sink.

"I'll see you tonight boo" He said looking down at his watch. He grabbed his briefcase from the counter top. "I'm taking you out tonight, so be ready around nine" He informed me.

"You're not going to finish eating?" I asked as I poked my fork into the plate of food.

"I've already eaten enough, and plus I have to run. I'm inducing a patient's labor at nine. Enjoy your breakfast"

He unarmed the house and was off to work... Again!

I arrived to work at exactly ten o' three. Three minutes after I was scheduled to be there. I dreaded going to work because I hated my job, and my rocky marriage, only made matters worse. I was reaching my breaking point with my place of employment and that damn hospital that seemed to take up all my husbands' time.

During my entire shift Jody was trying to figure out what was wrong with me, it was no secret that I was still in a foul mood about being alone on my anniversary and I guess he could sense the mood that I was in. Believe it or not sometimes I think that Jody knew me better than I knew myself. Although we'd just started working together we'd known each other for years. We were like family. His mother and my mother were best friends. Throughout my entire relationship with Terrence he'd been against it. Basically because every time he turned around I was telling him about some conniving bullshit that Terrence had done.

"Looks like somebody must have woken up on the wrong side of the bed this morning."

"Whateva! Okay. Today is not the day. TRUST!"

"Hello, how are you doing today mam" Jody said to a customer.

"I'm doing okay, glad to be alive...just need to get my blood pressure pills refilled."

"Let me see your ID please."

"Here you go sugar" The elderly lady said, as she handed Jody her identification.

"Thank you. I should have these ready for you in about thirty minutes."
The woman walked away.

"I have to go tinkle" Jody told me.

"Okay" I logged onto the computer not noticing that there was another customer standing in line.

"Hello beautiful" the guy said.
"Hello" I said without taking my eyes off the monitor.

"Do you treat all your customers this way or only the ones that call you beautiful"

"Girl he's a keeper" Jody whispered in my ear be fore he walked away.

He gets that way when he's attracted to someone. In case you haven't noticed, Jody is gay. You would be surprised by how many guys he screws around with. Most are married with families of their own. He's always whooping and hollering about somebody else's man. That's why I didn't pay any attention to him, or the aggravating ass customer.

I looked up. *Damn... He is sexy* I thought. Hoping I didn't say it out loud. "What do you mean?" I questioned him.

"Well you hadn't looked up until now"

I ignored his statement. "What can I help you with today sir?"

"I'm here to pick up a prescription for my son Marcus Barnes Jr."

"What's his birthday?"

"December 12, 2002"

I typed his information into the computer. "Your total is twenty five fourteen. Will you be paying with cash or card?"

"Cash" He handed me the cash. "Why are you looking so sad? What's a beautiful woman like you have to be sad about?"

In my mind I was saying *Damn this man is nosey as hell*. He resembled the NBA superstar D Wade only he was a little bit shorter.

"I've just had a long weekend"

"It can't be that bad- and if it is, I would love to have someone as beautiful as you to come home to at night." He smiled.

I smiled back. "You just had to throw some game in there didn't you?"

"That's not game. I'm only speaking the truth" He chuckled.

"Whateva! I bet you've told that to plenty of women"

"Nah. My lucks not that good. I've never crossed paths with a woman as cute as you before. Good to see you smile" He grabbed his package and headed on.

"Girl he was fine as hell. Why you ain't give 'em your number? He was definitely trying to get at cha'" Jody said as he approached the counter.

"Because I'm happily married"

"Well your happily married ass, needs to start coming to work in a better mood"

"I try but lately it seems that all Terrence does is piss me off"

"That's exactly why you should have given ol' boy your number. I don't know why you be stressing over that ignorant ass husband of yours. I bet he don't worry about his wedding band when women throw their ass at him, because if he cared about yall's marriage you wouldn't be so sad and crying all the time. I bet he don't cry over you."

"You don't know what you're talking about. Terrence has just been busy with work lately, that's all"

41

"Look. I don't care how busy he is. He should always make time for wifey. Instead of always making you feel like a burden"

"He doesn't make me feel like I'm a burden. Terrence makes sure that I'm well taken care of. I mean, he pays the bills, mortgage, and the car notes. He pays for all of our expenses. He's even the reason I got hired here."

"And? He's your husband. That's what he is supposed to do. Now does that mean that he's supposed to neglect you and control your life? Hell no! And what's all this talk about he's the reason that you got hired. Girl you hate this job. That asshole didn't even let you choose your own career. You need to stop letting that man control you"

"He doesn't control me. I make my own decisions. Terrence is right me having a dance studio is not a reliable source of income. So I chose a stable career. My husband knows what's best for me."

"He knows what's best for him. You didn't choose this career, he chose it for you. You know you do all this bragging, Terrence pays for this, Terrence pays for that, if he pays for everything it shouldn't matter how much money you bring into the house. That's just another excuse for your husband to regulate your life. I don't see how you put up with 'em.

"You're not in my marriage and that's why you need to stay the hell out of it."

"Wait a minute boo boo! Who in the hell do you think you snapping on? All I'm trying to say is you should never let a man handicap you to the point that you can't handle business without him. If Terrence leaves you today, he's going to leave you with nothing. No job, no car, no house, no money. Nothing.

"That's not something that's going to happen because Terrence and I vowed to death do us apart."

"And he made that same vow to his first wife. But my opinion doesn't matter. The only thing that matters is your happiness. You are happy right?

"Very. I guess. I mean things could be better but all relationships have its ups and downs."

"You just remember what I said. And don't be nobody's fool. Girl let me go clock out I got myself a hot date tonight. I still say you should have given ol' boy your number because it couldn't have been me. I would have given him my number quicker than a prisoner leaving the jailhouse grounds after getting released from doing a ten year bid."

"I bet you would" I laughed.

"See you later chic" He told me.

"Alright be safe"

I'm not going to lie; Jody was making some good points. But I shrugged him off and down played the whole conversation. I must admit, I'd been allowing Terrence to get away with murder.

6

TERRENCE

Luckily I was able to dodge Nicole during my entire shift on yesterday. That's why I drove the Rover instead of the Corvette to work again today. I don't want that crazy woman to know that I'm here. She's been blowing up my phone ever since we slept together. I mean damn, I broke her off some, why can't she just leave well enough alone. I knew I shouldn't have given her some of this good wood. Truth be told the only thing she can do for me now, is go down on me. And that might not even be a good idea. But it is tempting. She definitely knows what she's doing when it comes to oral sex. My intuition is telling me that Nicole is going to try and be on some relationship type of crap. And that's not going to work for me. The problem is, unlike the other women that I've fucked and forgot about, Nicole and I share the same employer and I know that I won't be able to avoid her for long.

The time has flown by, my shift is almost over and I've managed to stay clear from Nicole. I haven't received any emergency messages, and it looks like I'm going to be out of here on time. Finally, I can take my baby out tonight. My day is going well after all.

As I'm arranging things around in my office to make time suppress, Nicole barges in unannounced. After seeing how mad she looks, immediately I shut the door behind her.

"What kind of woman do you think I am?" She's standing a few inches away from me, in a deranged aura. She looks as though she wants to slap the living day lights out of me.

Afraid to answer the question truthfully, I reluctantly ask her. "What do you mean?"

"Oh don't patronize me, you left without a good-bye, and I know that you've seen my text messages and voice messages. I guess you got what you wanted. And that's it for us, huh?

"Got what I wanted? You are the one who practically threw yourself at me" I express maliciously.

"I don't recall you turning me down and being a faithful husband"

"It's none of your business, the kind of husband I am to my wife; you don't need to worry about my marriage"

"Oh, don't worry I'm not worried about your marriage, but you're gonna' be as soon as I tell your wife about us."

Before I could respond to Nicole's remark my mobile starts to ring. I walk away, and stand alone before I answer.

"Hey what's up?"

"Are we still going out tonight?"

"I'm finishing up things now and I'll be home shortly, be ready when I get there"

"Okay, I was just making sure, because I'm on my way home from work. I wanted to be sure that I didn't need to stop and grab me a bite to eat. See you when you get home. Love Ya."

"Love you to" I hang up, and place my phone back into my coat pocket.

"Oh you love her, huh?"

What kind of a question is that? This woman is psycho. She is on some Thin Line Between Love and Hate shit. That has to be the dumbest question I've ever been asked. I'm not going to entertain her crazy ass. And I am definitely not going to say something to piss her off any more than she already is, because if I do she'll try to find out everything that she possibly can about Alexis, and run straight to her to tell her every damn thing. So for the most part I play it cool insuating that her behavior is not fazing me at all.

In a low tone I ask. "Why would you tell my wife, what has she done to you? You knew I was married when you willingly shared your secrets with me"

"I knew that you were married, but I didn't expect for you to treat me this way"

"Treat you like what?" I ask her knowing exactly what she means.

"Well for one you're avoiding me...screening my calls. I thought you were going to be different from all the others." Her eyes begin to get watery.

"Don't cry" I console her and hand her a Kleenex. "You'll meet a man that's good for you. But I can't be that man" I walk away from her and continue straightening things around my office.

"Please don't say that" She begs and trots behind me. She reaches around me and grabs my dick. "Wasn't it good? Don't you want some more?" She says as she rubs her hands up my chest.

I turn around to her. Her blouse is now unbuttoned. "Look, stop! This can't go on. You have to stop" I mandate as I push her away. Quickly she buttons her blouse and straightens her clothes. "What's wrong with you" I holler.

She's proves to me how crazy she really is by knocking my wife's picture off of my desk. Now she's grabbed a glass vase, and a few other items that help accessorize my office. "What in the hell are you doing?" I shout. She ignores me and throws them viciously into the wall.

7

ALEXIS

"Hello…hello…helloooo" I said repeatedly as I answered my mobile, but there was no response. "*He needs to learn to lock his phone when he isn't using it. Every time I turn around that phone is calling me.*" I mumbled to myself as I waited for the traffic light to turn green. Just as I was about to hang up I heard Terrence say.

"Look you need to pull yourself together, your starting to come off as a crazy woman"

I turned down the radio and before I knew it I'd driven off while the light was red, and almost collided with another vehicle. The woman driving made sure that I knew that she was pissed, when she honked her horn and called me everything but a child of God. I sped forward.

"I wasn't so crazy the other night when we fucked. I bet your wife would love to know the truth about where you were the other night."

I questioned myself. *What? Did I just hear what I think I heard? Did another woman just say she fucked my husband?* Distraught by what I'd heard, I didn't realize that the car ahead of me had slowed down. I slammed on the brakes, screeching my tires. And a burning sensation traveled through my entire body. I was so furious that I didn't know what to do. A huge knot formed in the pit of my stomach as I pictured my husband, being intimate with someone other than me.

"Look I'm tired of your little threats, I'm not worried about your threats okay, and my marriage is not threatened. My wife is not going to believe a word that you tell her because I'm going to deny it all. Now get the hell out of my office."

I heard a noise that sounded like glass was being broken before the female that Terrence had obviously cheated on me with, yelled bitterly "Fuck your wife, your marriage and this damn office because when I'm done with you, you want have any of them" I heard a door slam.

"Your marriage is not threatened huh? Well... we'll just have to see about that." I said amongst myself as I pressed END on my mobile. Immediately I called em' back but as usual this is what I heard. You have reached the voice the mailbox of six seven eight blah-blah- blah. You know the rest. Trifling ass men!

I drove home running traffic lights, stop signs, yield signs and all in between. I pulled into the driveway hopped out of the truck, and went into the house. It was time for some sweet revenge. I had something for dat ass! How could he have the balls to be sleeping around on our anniversary? *Why did I believe his lying ass?* constantly swirled around in my head. *"Work my ass"* I blurted out. *"He was at work alright, busy working another bitch!"* I said out loud. Stumping around the house once again, but this time I was searching for the ammonia. Revenge was all I could imagine.

What I'd just heard was heartbreaking. I always heard he was screwing around on me. But I never had the proof. So I believed what I wanted to believe. Never acknowledging the fact that my husband was the ho' of all ho's. And now that I'd finally heard it with my own ears from the horse's mouth, I could no longer lie to my-self. You best believe that I had something in store for his grimy ass.

"Baby, are you ready?" Terrence yelled up the stairs as he walked into the house.

The sound of his voice alone was pissing me off. I gritted my teeth and in the calmest tone that I could speak, I yelled back "Come up here for a second"

He jogged up the staircase. "You're not ready to go? I told you to be ready when I got here" he said as he walked into the bedroom and noticed that I was still dressed in my work uniform.

"Come here I have something to show you" I grabbed his hand and escorted him into the bathroom"

"I don't see anything" He puzzled.

And that's when I grabbed the bucket that I'd filled up with ammonia and dashed it into his face.

"What in the fuck did you do that for?

"You ought to be glad that I didn't chop your dick off with you nasty ass"

"What did you put in that water? My eyes are burning"

"It's not water, Stupid. Its ammonia. Your eyes oughta' burn and if you keep fucking every woman that you meet your dick is going to burn to."

"Hand me a wet towel I can't see"

"I' don't give a damn about you not being able to see and I'm not handing you shit."

"Woman… Why are you acting damn crazy?"

"I know where you were on our anniversary"

"What are you talking about? I told you I was at work" He told me right before he jetted over to the sink.

"That's bullshit and you know it. You were with another woman and I heard everything that I needed to hear. Because your STUPID ASS didn't have your phone locked. Your phone called me earlier and I heard the entire argument between you and the bitch. I bet it's one of the chic's that works with you. Isn't It.?" I asked taking off my shoe so that I could hit him with it.

"I don't know what you talking about" He says rinsing out his eyes with cold water and flinching as I repeatedly hit him with my shoe.

"You know what hang it up. Quit fucking lying." I wailed giving him an evil glare.

After I repeated to him the whole conversation that I heard word for word, the only thing that he could do was stand there and look stupid, while he held a wet wash cloth over his left eye.

"Look at cha' now looking like a damn fool" I pointed out as I turned my back to him and exited the bathroom. I walked into the closet so that I could collect a few pieces of clothing.

"I'm sorry baby" Terrence pleaded with teary eyes. "Where are you going?"

"I'm going to be staying over at Lisa's place until I can find a place of my own." I ranted as I moved quickly from the closet to the bed with pieces of my clothing.

"Lexi please, hit me, curse at me, I don't care what you do. Please don't leave me" Terrence begged tugging at my arm.

I pushed him away "Get out of my damn way" I grabbed my luggage chunked it onto the bed and stuffed my clothes inside. "Ask the woman who you were with the other night to come over here with you. Better yet ask her to marry you and put up with all your bullshit, because this marriage is over."

"I mess up once and you're just going to leave me?"

I was standing there with my luggage in tow. "Whatever Terrence your ass been doing shit this entire marriage, this is just the first time that you've gotten caught."

"Please don't leave we can work it out. I need you, I can't breathe without you"

"Well you better get use to it; because you will not ever taste these juices again. Let me ask you something. You think that guys don't come on to me?"

"What you trying to say? You're cheating."

"No, but I should have. Unlike you I have respect for our marriage" I sighed heavily as I wiggled my wedding ring off of my finger. "I guess I want be needing this anymore" I handed him my ring and whimpered "Goodbye Terrence"

Terrence followed behind me down the staircase begging for me to stay, asking me to give him a second chance. I didn't give him the satisfaction. I left him there looking like a sad puppy. That was the first time that I left Terrence, but it was only the beginning of a marriage full of good sex, money, and heartache.

8

TERRENCE

Damn, I miss her like crazy. I never speculated that my skeletons would come out of the closet. I presumed that I could do whatever I wanted to do. Stay out as long as I wanted to. Fuck however many women I wanted to fuck, and as long as I took care of her she'd always be here. She gotta' brother fucked up right now. I'm calling her job, begging her back, riding by Lisa's house ten, twelve times a day. How strange was it that my phone called her accidentally in the midst of an argument with Nicole's crazy ass? There was no way that I could try to lie, my way out of that one. She heard every damn thing, it would have taken some hellofva' convincing to get her to believe that she didn't hear what she heard. For the last two weeks, I've, been, looking at my phone every time that it rings hoping that it's my baby. But it never is. She won't return my calls, so I have only been able to leave and send messages. I gotta' get her back, because I can't afford to go through another divorce. My first wife walked away with more than I wanted to give her ass. I learned the hard way; that's it's cheaper to keep her.

I haven't been to work since the last quarrel that I got into with Stupido-Stupido being Nicole. I'm so sick and tired of her sending me crazy ass text messages and voicemail messages. I'm really thinking about taking out a restrainer order on her. She sends threatening text messages about my wife, my job, me and anything else that involves me. The helfa calls me or texts me every five minutes. Speaking of the devil, she's texting me at this moment. *Terrence I told you I can be a crazy bitch but I guess you didn't believe me. I know where your wife gets her hair done and when I catch her there, I got something for her ass. Looks like you picked the wrong woman to sleep with.*

I nod my head after reading the first part of the text message before I'm interrupted by my mother calling.

"Hello mama"

"Hi baby: Not going to hold you long: I've got something to tell you, and I don't know where to start."

I settle into my bed. She's calling to vent. And most of the time when she calls, she's calling with news that I don't necessarily care about. Either my brother has been locked up again, or she hasn't heard from him in a few days. Then she'll start to complain about how he's been running her blood pressure up and how she is not going to let him come back this time. If she's not calling about something that's pertaining to Terry, this will be a first.

So what if Terry has been locked up again. Good. Maybe she can relax and stop worrying about what his- up to no good behind- is doing for a few days.

"Terrence? Are you listening to me? Are you busy?

"No mama, but hold on for a sec, I've got a call coming through."
I pressed the TALK button. "Hello"

"Why haven't I been able to reach you? Your son needs some money. And why haven't you been by to see him?"

"Well hello to you too. I'm coming by to see him today. And I just sent you two thousand dollars two weeks ago; a baby can't go through two thousand dollars in two weeks"

"Look, you best be glad that I haven't taken your ass to court for child support, because I, can, get more than that. And another thing you lucky I haven't told your wife that you've been cheating on her with me and that we have a two year old son together."

"Look, I'll call you back my mother is on the other line"

"Terrence..."

I hung up without giving her the chance to finish her sentence. Every time that we talk it's always about money...money...money...and more money. I don't understand how she goes through so much money. Then she always throws it up in my face how she can spill the

56

beans and tell Alexis everything. If Alexis and I get back together, which I'm sure that we will. I may come clean about everything. I'm sick and tired of her holding that over my head.

"Mama"

"Yeah sugga"

"Sorry about that, that was an old friend, so, what's up mama?"

"I don't know how to start, but your daddy…"
She started to cry and her voice began to tremble.

"What's wrong with pop ma? What's wrong?"

"He had a heart attack and passed away today"
All of a sudden my heart began to speed up a mile a minute. Not my pop… not the man that worked his ass off for his family. My pops and I are closer than two chicks that have fucked the same man, and yet managed to stay friends. And now he's gone. *Why…Lord why?*

I constrain my emotions of anguish, and somehow I occlude myself from crying. I know that I have to be strong for my mother who is sobbing on the other end of the phone

"Mama, don't cry everything is going to be okay."

"I'm trying to stay strong baby. But what am I going to do without him? What am I going to do? Who's going to protect me?"

"I'm going to be there for you mama. I'm going to take care of you"

"I've been with that man for fifty five years. He was a good father, a good cook, a good husband, a provider, a friend, a confidante, and now he's gone. Why? Why my husband? She cries.

"Mama Calm down before I end up having to bury two parents. Mama… after the funeral, I think that it's best if you move in with me"

"What about Terry?"

"Mama Terry is a grown man that needs to learn to take care of himself. He's probably the one that sent daddy to an early grave"

"Don't talk about your brother like that" She dictates.

"I'm sorry mama. I didn't mean to say that. I'm not trying to get you upset at a time like this. You try to relax and I'm going to go ahead and book my flight for tomorrow night. I have something I need to take care of first."

"Okay baby. Love ya." She whimpered.

"Love you to mama"

We both hung up the phone. I held myself together pretty good while I was on the phone with my mother. But now that we've hung up I'm crying like a hungry newborn. I can't believe that my old man is gone. I can't believe it!

9

ALEXIS

Can you believe it? After all the planning I did and the hard work I put into our anniversary. He had the audacity to leave me home alone, while he was with another woman. For the life of me, I couldn't get the image of my husband making love to another woman out of my head.

I was so sick and tired of his ass begging and begging for me to come back home! It was true; you never miss your water until your well runs dry. I had always told Terrence that one day all his lies would catch up with him, but he never listened to me. All those nights that I begged him to talk about our problems he never had time or he was always too tired. It's funny how the tables had turned around, because now he wanted to talk but I was the one without the time to listen.

I decided to take one of my personal days, because I was in desperate need of a touch up. My new growth was screaming, save me. I knew good in well I should have been in somebody's salon weeks ago. So I called Lisa to find out if she had any openings. After she told me that she could squeeze me in I arrived at the shop about 30 minutes later dressed down wearing some sweat pants, a white tee shirt, and a pair of sneakers. When I walked through the door I noticed these two women were eyeing me down. "What in the hell is there problem" I thought to myself, but I managed to remain a lady and walked to the seats beside them and sat down.

"Go to the back Alexis and let Nikki wash your hair"

"I'm in desperate need of a touch up"

"It hasn't been 8 weeks since you last had a touch up" Lisa said, walking over to me. She began running her hands through my scalp." You need to wait a couple of weeks you only need a wash"

"Are you sure about that?"

"Girl after I flat iron your hair, I promise you that you won't know the difference"

"Okay we'll see" I told her.

I walked away headed to the shampoo room. Apparently while I was in the back the two women up front must have not known that Lisa and I were best friends because they were sitting up their talking about me right in front of her. Saying things like. *That's the bitch whose husband I fucked.*" You know. Laughing like something was hilarious. And that's why Lisa came into the shampoo room.

"Promise me that when I tell you this; you won't go off in here?" Lisa asked.

"I promise. Now what is going on?"

"Those two women up there are talking about you and one of them is claiming that she's screwed Terrence."

I rose up from the shampoo bowl with water and suds everywhere and ran to the front of the shop where the two women were. "Which one of you is fucking my husband?"

"I'm the one that's fucked your husband. You know, the night that he didn't come home."

One woman said while standing with her arms folded. What in the hell did Terrence see in that helfa? I mean, she looked alright. My face looked better and my ass was bigger. I was relieved once I stood face to face with the woman that my husband had cheated on me with, because that bitch couldn't hold a candle to me.

"What will you get out of sleeping with a married man?"

"Nothing but good dick, vacations, and his money" she giggled.

"Oh it's funny to you? We'll see how funny it is when I kick your ass."

Hearing what the woman had just told me put me in another place. I was outside of myself because I then pushed the woman so hard down to the floor it sounded like one of her bones had broken.

"Bitch" she called out to me.

"You are the bitch. You thought I was going to let you say all that shit to me and I wasn't going to do anything about it?" I yelled while giving her a couple of blows to the forehead.

I was on top of her beating the hell out of her ass and that's when her friend jumped in, and started choking me from behind. This gave her the chance to get up and the next thing I knew the two of them were stumping the hell out of me until a couple of guys from the back came in and broke up the fight.

"This shit ain't over" I said as I was being helped off the floor.

"I stay ready. Bitch!" She snapped back.

My face was bruised and the muscles in my stomach were so sore from getting stumped, that I could barely make it to my vehicle.

Back in my truck the only thing that I could do was cry. *How did I get here*? I questioned myself. I had never gotten into a fight before in my whole life. What was up with me? And to top it off, things just seemed to be getting worse that day, because my truck would not crank. What else could go wrong? After I tried to start the engine of my Rover a few more times, I called a towing service.

Waiting for the tow truck to get there seemed like forever. I didn't have time to be sitting there all day and I was too embarrassed to go back inside the salon. I just wanted to ring Terrence's neck. Not only had I just gotten into a brawl with a woman over 'em but he told me that he'd taken my car for a tune up only a few weeks earlier. Now either he lied about having it serviced, or whatever mechanic serviced the truck didn't know what in the hell they were doing. It just turned out to be a bad day all the way around. Because what I went to Lisa for, didn't get done-which explained why I was sitting there with a plastic cap on my head-looking worse than I did when I got there. After the fight, I was not up for a hair-do anymore. And who could blame me?

"It's about time they got here. Oh Lord not today!" I said all in the same sentence, realizing that the guy driving the tow truck was the same guy that I'd met at work a few weeks back.

"You called for towing service" He said as he strided up to my vehicle.

I was hoping that he didn't recognize me. Especially, since I had a slightly blackened eye and a cut across my bottom lip. "Yes. And it took you long enough to get here"

"Calm down beautiful. You know the traffic is crazy in Atlanta… You didn't think that I would recognize you, did you?"

"Nah." I nodded my head. "I'm surprised that you realize who I am"

"How could I forget a face that pretty?"

"There you go again" I laughed.

He laughed. "Where are you getting your vehicle towed to? And who are you going to let take a look at it?"

"I'm getting it towed to my friend's house and I don't know who's going to fix it just yet."

"I'll take a look at it for you; I have my own mechanic shop"

"First, how much is this going to cost me, and secondly I'll have to think about it"

"Okay, while you think about it, just know that for you it's free of charge"

"Nothing in life is free I'll have to pay you something"

"Just let me take you out"

"That's not a good idea"

"Why is that? He asked opening the door so that I could get out.

"Because I'm a married woman" I said stepping out of my vehicle.

"Okay...Beautiful and faithful. I like." He complimented, as he shut the door. "Let me get everything set to go and we will be ready to head to the shop in no time."

"What do you mean, we?"

"You are going to ride with me right?"

"I guess" I told him as if I was unsure.

He walked off to get busy hooking the two vehicles together. I opened the door to the tow truck and hopped in. After about five minutes he leaped into the truck.

"Why is it that every time I see you it seems as though you are so sad? He asked as he positioned his rearview mirror.

"I'm just going through a lot right now "

"I wish you would realize how wonderful you are and put all the nonsense in your life aside."

"It's not that simple"

"Of course it is all you have to do is let go and let God." He recognized that I was struggling to buckle the seat belt. Let me help you with that" He worded. As he snapped the buckle he got a better look at my face. "What happened to your face" He asked looking concerned.

"What station is this" I asked trying to avoid his question.

"Don't change the subject. Is your husband beating on you?"

"No he isn't beating on me" I answered trying to hold back the tears. "I got into a fight with a woman my husband was cheating on me with and her friend jumped in."

"Whoa! How did you get yourself in that kind of a situation?"

"I really don't want to talk about that right now, will you just pull off already. The quicker we get this over with. The quicker I'll be able to get back home"

"Your husband must be beating himself upside the head for messing up like that?" He questioned as he put the truck in the first gear and drove into the traffic lane.

"He should be, he needs to hurt all the shit he puts me through"

"How long have ya'll been married?

"3 years"

"Why have you stayed with him for so long if he's taking you through hell?"

"Because I love him"

"Are you sure that's what it is? Or is that you've just gotten so use to living the good life that you can't see yourself going back to living a normal life? You can always love someone else just the same, if not more. I learned the hard way a long time ago that money, jewelry and flashy cars are not worth risking your happiness." What does your husband do for a living?"

"He's a doctor"

"Well I hope that he's smart enough to realize that he has something good before it's too late, money can only buy happiness for a little while"

"What do you mean by that?"

"I have a feeling that you know exactly what I mean."

Marcus was exactly right; I was tired of the gifts, the trips, and cars that were only bought to substitute for love. I needed affection...romance...love letters, I wanted to be happy in my marriage.

I remained quiet the remainder of the drive to Marcus' shop.

I was sore and I wasn't really in the mood for sitting there while Marcus tried to figure out what was going on with my Rover. That's why it was never serviced unless

Terrence had taken it for me. Which is probably the reason why I was sitting there squirming in the uncomfortable chair, not knowing what was wrong with it. His lying ass probably never took it in the first place.

I was reading magazines, mainly about- how to lose weight -ten ways to keep your man happy- celebrities, and so on. Not even realizing that I'd been sitting there for two hours and I still didn't know what was wrong with my Rover. Marcus had walked past the lobby about twenty times and hadn't told me a thing.

"Excuse me" I said loud enough to get his attention once I'd glanced up and spotted him walking by the lobby again.

"Yeh"

"Have you found out what the problem is yet?"

"I was just about to come over and tell you what the problem is. We found a major problem. You have a leak coming from your transmission, and that's only part of the problem. It's going to take a little longer than we thought. I'll take you home and have one of the guys drop it off to you tomorrow"

"I guess I don't have a choice. It's either that or I wait here, even longer for a cab to get here" I said hesitantly.

"Okay then. That's wutz up'. I'll meet you outside in a few minutes."

"Okay. And thanks for everything"

"No problem" He assured me.

Moments later we headed to Lisa's house.

10

TERRENCE

Since earlier today I've been sitting in front of Lisa's house hoping that I can catch Alexis. My good friend Christopher, who is her district Manager told me that she'd requested today off, and since I've been waiting on her to arrive for about two hours now, she should be getting here soon. She doesn't run the streets…So where can she be? I don't know what in the hell could be taking her so long to get here. I really need someone to talk to. I'm a mess right now. Yesterday I found out that my dad passed. Nicole is stalking me. Janice is demanding money, which is another problem that I brought on myself. I just don't know what to do. I do know that I want to save our marriage. Alexis and I don't need to spend another night away from each other. Just like the sudden death of my dad. One of us can be here today and gone tomorrow. So we need to have a serious conversation about what we plan on doing to salvage our marriage. Because it would be nice to know where we stand before I catch my flight to Missouri tonight. It would be even nicer if my Lexi Pooh would come with me. Given our circumstances, I think that it's safe to say that, that would be a stretch. I miss her smile, her laugh; I even miss her calling me a lying black bastard. Right now I'll take anything that I can get.

I can't stand the thought of her possibly being with a man other than me. That's how I know that I must do whatever it takes to get her back into our bedroom. Either that, or watch her grow old with another man. That thought really doesn't sit well with me at all. I can't stand for her to talk to another man, because I know what he's thinking in the back of his head. So to think that it could possibly be over between us, and another man will have the chance to make love to her, is driving me crazy.

I'm almost about to reverse my car and back out of the driveway when I look into my rearview mirror and see that a tow truck is pulling up behind me. My day couldn't be any worse because I recognize that the woman sitting on the passenger side of the truck is Alexis.

"So that's why you want to give up on our marriage?" I roar as I get out of my car and slam the door shut.

"Your bullshit is the reason why I want to give up on this marriage"

"You fucking him?"

"Yeh Terrence I just met him, and I'm already fucking him" Alexis says sarcastically.

"You fucking my wife?" I imply banging on the side of the tow truck.

"You keep beating on my truck like that and you are going to be a doctor going to the doctor with broken bones".

"Well get your ass out of the truck then... And you!" I grabbed the door handle. "Get your ass out Alexis" I opened the door and snatched Alexis out of the truck.

"I got better shit to do with my time then to be going to jail for whipping your ass... Aye you don't need to be pulling on her like that"

"Don't try to tell me how to handle my wife"

"Terrence you're hurting my arm"

"You shouldn't be riding around in his goddamn truck" I pull her by the arm as we walk up the steps to Lisa's house.

The asshole reverses, and drives off, leaving me and Alexis standing outside Lisa's house arguing for the next hour and a half. After a long debate of whether Alexis has been messing around during our marriage or not I'm really not that convinced that she's telling the truth. How can she say that she just met the guy when the asshole knows that I am a doctor? And why did she tell him our business anyway?

"This is some foul shit that you're doing Alexis, how in the hell can you talk all that shit about me, but you riding around with another man?"

"I'm not seeing that man, he's doing the maintenance on my truck, and there is a lot of work that needs to be done to it; so he's keeping it overnight."

"What does that have to do with you riding in the car with him?"

"I didn't have a way here, and he offered to give me a ride."

"Well I bet he had something else in mind."

"Not every man thinks like you"

"You taking up for him now"

"Whateva' Terrence! I'm not in the mood to argue right now" Alexis says as she twists the doorknob to Lisa's apartment"

I grabbed her by the arm "If I find out that you been messing around on me with that low class, broke ass, piece of a shitty ass man, I'm going to hurt both of you"

"You're hurting me" Alexis screams as she tries to break away from me. "What in the hell is wrong with you threatening me like this?

"I'm sorry baby," I tell her releasing my grip once again. "I just hate the idea of you being with someone other than me."

"Well how do you think I felt when the woman at the hair salon told me, she fucked you on our anniversary?" She pauses for a quick second. "You don't have anything to say now do you. She pushes open the door and walks in, and then she turns around and looks at me through the glass door, with the saddest expression I've ever seen on her face.

"Will you just come back home so that we can try and work things out" I ask her sincerely.

"I need some time to think things through"

"Please, I miss you. I also want------

"You- You-You, everything is always about you. Look, I'm too tired to deal with this right now"

She slammed the door in my face. So I have no choice but to give her some space and I guess I'm going to be attending my pops funeral without her after all, because she didn't give me the chance to tell her about the tragic news.

11

ALEXIS

Back in the house, I took out the business card that Marcus had given me when I got out of his car, and dialed his number.

"Hello" he answered with a very deep voice. *Damn he sounds good on the phone* I thought to myself. "Are you busy?"

"Not at the moment"

"I just wanted to call and apologize for the way my husband acted towards you"

"That wasn't your fault; you're not, responsible for his actions."

"I've never seen him act that way"

"That's how some men get when they know that they've messed things up with a good woman."

"I'm just glad things didn't get out of pocket."

"Oh they could have, but out of respect for you, I managed to keep my cool,' but the next time I might not be so calm."

"It won't happen again"

"I wouldn't be so sure about that" Marcus responded. He changed the subject "That house that I took you to…does King Pen live there?

"Yeh"

"Are you two related?"

"No he's married to my best friend?

"How do you know King Pen?" I questioned.

"It's a long story… let's just say that we go way back. But let me get back to work so that I can have your ride ready by tomorrow"

"Sweet dreams" he said before he hung up the phone.

Once I'd apologized and was sure that Marcus wasn't bothered by Terrence's ecstatic behavior I took a hot shower. Afterwards I started to call Terrence and tell him that I needed to borrow his Corvette, at least until I could get the Rover back, but I decided against it because I didn't want to hype him all up into thinking, that this meant I was ready to move back home just yet. I definitely didn't want to give him any reason to think that his ass was out of the clear with me, so I hung up my cellular and went into the kitchen with Moesha and Lisa.

Moesha is Lisa's younger sister. Her name should have been Hoesha. She has five kids, by five different guys. And her last baby's daddy swore that he was a hustla' but his ass didn't have a vehicle. How can you call yourself a hustla' and not have a car?

"Who in the hell was that good looking man you were in the car with? And what was Terrence yelling about? Moesha asked not even giving me the chance to sit down good. Her nosey ass must have been looking out the window.

"That was Marcus he's going to be doing some mechanical work on my vehicle. And Terrence was just being an asshole as usual"

"He's always being an asshole" Lisa followed. She was putting a relaxer in Moesha's hair.

"Well are you going to fuck him?" Moesha wanted to know.

"Who?"

"Mr. Sexy" She joked.

"No. I'm a married woman."

"Terrence didn't think about that" Lisa commented.

"Two wrongs don't make a right" I argued.

"It doesn't, but it will make you feel better" Moesha joked.

"It's funny how you hate my husband now Lisa, when the two of you were friends before I met him"

"Would you respect my husband if he did half the shit to me that Terrence does to you?"

I overlooked her question and asked. "So I take it that two of you will think that I'm stupid if I take Terrence back?"

"Hell yeh! Fuck his ass; I wouldn't be putting up with all his bullshit" Moesha said quickly.

"I'm not going to voice my opinion because you're going to do what you want to do anyway." Lisa remarked.

After hearing their comments I became upset and I'm sure that they could tell based on my sudden change of tone. "How can you fix your mouth to say that when you've been on a roller coaster ride with Tony for two years and he's a fucking bomb?" I snapped at Moesha.

"My situation is a little different from yours, because I have five children. I'm lucky that he wants to be with me. Even though he is a damn sorry ass wannabe' hustla'. I gotta' take what I can get. But you don't have to, you don't have any kids, and you a dime with a phat ass, you can have any man you want"

"People always seem to tell me that, but I don't want anyone but Terrence"
Lisa rolled her eyes as she shook her head back and forth.

"Well take him back then, and don't worry about what people have to say about it. Hell, people are going to talk anyway." Moesha felt the need to say.

"My heart is saying take 'em back, but my head is telling me that he's never going to change"

"Realistically speaking, he won't. He never does. He's always going to be the cheating asshole that he is" Lisa blurted.

I ignored her. "So, do you think I should call 'em Moesha?"

"If I were you, I wouldn't, I would let his ass suffer for a little bit longer, but hey, you gotta' do you boo."

"Girl, I miss him like crazy."

We talked for a little bit longer until I received a call from my mother, and excused myself from the kitchen. I went into the guest-room. Later, I thought about all the advice that Moesha and Lisa had given me and I remember mumbling to myself *"Hell, he's my husband I can take him back however many times I want to."* My mind was made up; I was going to go back to Terrence after I made him miss me a little longer.

I wanted to jump into his arms when were outside, but I didn't want to give in so easy. Seeing his reaction when I pulled up with Marcus was a turn on for me.

So I continued to avoid his calls and texts for the next week. I called myself teaching him a lesson. What was his lesson? That he'd better think twice before he cheated on me again!

12

TERRENCE

After being away from home for a week, I'm on a plane flying back to GA without my mother. I did my best to convince her to leave Missouri and move in with me, but she wasn't trying to hear it. My mother worries to much about my brother. And the only thing that he worries about is how he's going to get his next high. I believe my mother knows it to, no matter how naïve she pretends to be. Every time that I turn around she's asking me if I'll wire her some money, because she's misplaced a few dollars. She always says. *"I don't know where I put that money sugga, I laid it down somewhere"* I know deep down she knows that her money is going toward her son's drug addiction. Who else could be taking her money? But I have more important business to worry about. First thing first, I must find a way to come clean about everything; secondly, I must put Janice in her place, and last but not least, it's urgent that I take a restrainer order out on Nicole.

I don't know how in the hell that crazy woman found out where I live, but as I step out of the cab, my car is sitting on four bricks, with all the windows shattered, and a note attached to it. HELLO MR. WAM-BAM-THANK YOU-MAM NOW I'VE FUCKED UP BOTH OF YOUR BABIES SINCERELY YOURS, BITCH.

So what do I do? I call the cops. The officer laughs after I give him the rundown of what happened between Nicole and me, and why I suspect that she is the person that vandalized my Corvette. He jots everything down and hands me a police department mission statement with the case report number listed on it and tells me that the actual report will be available in twenty four hours.

Now if that's not fatal attraction, I must not know what fatal attraction is. She's attacked my wife, destroyed my vehicle, and threatened to tell my boss what happened between us. What else is she going to do? I've got to put a stop to this nutcase because wheneva' Alexis comes back home she's definitely not going to put up with this bullshit.

Later, I go to the dealership and buy another vehicle. And when Alexis asks me...*why?* I'll just tell her that it's her anniversary present.

I guess all my days of fucking around is finally catching up with me, and is about to bite me in my ass, because Nicole is not the biggest problem that I have. I was stupid enough to get another woman knocked up and now she too-is threatening my ass. That scares me, because out of all the grimy things that I've done during this marriage. I'll be the first to say that fathering a baby with another woman was downright wrong

As I'm napping I hear *Ring...Ring.* I roll over and grab my mobile off of the night stand beside the bed. I glance at the number. *"I'll call her back later"* I say. I hit the ignore button and lay back down. *Ring...Ring* I hear it again. I sit up, stretch and grab my phone. It's Janice again. I answer.

"What's up with you" I say trying not to sound frustrated.

"Being broke! What happened to you? I thought you were going to come by and bring some money for your son"

"I got side tracked after my mother called and told me that my pops had passed. I'm just getting back from Missouri"

"Sorry that your family had to go through that. But you have a son over here that's in need of some serious cash right now"

"Why don't you just say it? You're the one that needs some money, not T.J."

"Okay, well if it makes you feel better, I need some money"

"Look Janice, you're going to have to start slowing down, you're going through way too much money. From now on when T.J. needs something I'll go out and buy it for him"

"Oh, hush. You got that long money, your pockets ain't hurting. That's not the way it's going to go, I want the money"

Before I could strike back after what Janice said to me I hear a loud shatter coming from downstairs. I run downstairs to deactivate the alarm system before it awakes the entire neighborhood. I glance out the window and spot Nicole getting in her car before she speeds off. See what I'm talking about? Do you see how crazy she is? She just busted my living room window in broad fucking day light, if she's trying to push my buttons to get my attention, she's definitely caught my eye but it's not the kind of attention she's hoping for. I'm getting real close to kicking a woman's ass for the first time in my life.

"Hello" Janice starts to yell.

"Yeh I'm here"

"Well are you coming by today are not"

"How much money you need?" I'm tampering with the broken window.

"About two grand"

"Hell nah, I'm bringing you six hundred dollars and that should keep you straight until next week."

"Terrence… Six hundred dollars! Who in the hell do you think I am? You must think that I'm one of them dumb chicken heads that you mess around with. If you come…no, when you come, you best have more than six hundred dollars."

Hearing her, say that to me with everything that I'm going through right now forces me to erupt like a fucking volcano. That last remark, confirms that she thinks that I'm her personal bank account. For two years I've pampered her with more money than I can keep up with. Don't get me wrong, I'm all for taking care of my son, but not her sorry ass. Ever since she gave birth to my son, she hasn't worked. The only thing she does is sit on her ass, and use my son as her goddamn piggy bank. It's got to stop.

"Janice, if you want more than what I'm agreeing to give you, you're going to have to get off your sorry ass and work for it"

"What did you just say? I'm a single mother, if I work who's going to take care of our son"

"Hell. Put him in child care, you get more than enough money. At least then I'll know where my money is going"

"Kiss my ass; you sorry excuse for a father. You'd be able to give me more money if you stop lacing your boogey ass wife with diamonds and spending all your money buying new cars.

"I'll pass on kissing your ass, that's what's got me into this situation with your money hungry ass in the first place. And how do you know that I have a new car?"

"As if I don't see you driving it"

"I just got the damn car today"

"Look never mind how I know that you have a new car, you need to start spending more time with your son"

"What do you want me to do? I spend time with T.J., You just thought that I was going to leave my wife for you, and pretend that you, T.J and I are a happy family."

"Fuck you, you black bastard! Call me what you want. A ho', a gold-digger, a sorry ass woman but remember this, at the end of the day, I'm one more thing. And that's your child's mother."

Click.

She hung up on me. I'm glad to. Her calling for thousands of dollars is starting to get old. I'm not going to keep giving her that type of money so that she can feed her sorry ass, and then save the left overs for my son. As much money I've given that woman in the last two years she should have a nice car, and a decent house. Instead she's still catching the bus and living in section eight housing. When I met her she had goals. I mean the woman has a bachelor degree in business, there is no reason she should just be sitting around depending on money from me to survive.

13

JANICE

"Girl his black ass is as selfish as they come" I vent to Nicole as I run on the treadmill. We're at the gym, and we've been here for a few hours. I called her to meet me here, immediately after I hung up the phone with Terrence

"Who?" Nicole wants to know. "If you ask me they all are" She breathes heavily, as she continues to run on the treadmill that's adjacent to me.

"I'm talking about my stupid ass sperm donor, that's who. Because he sure is not, what I would call a father"

Nicole chuckles, before she says "I told your ass to let the child support services handle everything the legal way, but no you want to take it easy on him and do everything his way."

"Go to hell, Nicole. I'm not like you. I'm not the one to send threatening text messages, and burst out car windows. That's just not my thing. You keep doing those types of things to guys and you're going to be in a world of trouble."

"I don't give a damn men should think before they fuck me and suddenly catch a case of amnesia afterwards."

"So what, are you just going to keep torturing these guys until you get yourself hurt?"

"If you're asking me if I'm going to continue fucking up your baby daddy's life, I'm not. I'm done. I've done what I wanted to do. I didn't miss my period, which means that I'm not pregnant. So now I'm on to the next one."

"I slipped up and told Terrence that I knew he had a new car"

Nicole pauses the momentum on the treadmill. "You did what?"

"Relax, he didn't put two and two together"

"Thank God! So what are you going to do to get his ass back?" She presses the START button on the treadmill and continues running.

"I don't know Nicole; you know that I don't usually do things like this. What do you suggest?"

"First, you need to send him a text message stating that you need some money for TJ. Girl you know that helfa is going through his call log, and his messages, because she doesn't trust his ass. And the only thing that he is going to do is deny everything and that's when you put the icing on the cake and show up at her job."

"Terrence is going to be pissed"

"Who cares? That's why you're venting right...Because he's done something to piss you off?"

"You're right! Why should I care about how pissed he's going to be? He doesn't care about me. Pay back is a bitch and I'm her right hand girl." I giggle.

She and I both turn off the treadmills. We step off of them and begin stretching. We take a five minute break, drink a bottle of water, and begin exercising again.

Mad is an understatement to try and describe the mood that I am in at the moment. Even though I know that 80% of what Terrence said to me was the truth, I still want to play dirty and make him pay for being an asshole. My evil side is fucking with my good side and I'm not going to feel better until I break even with scandalous ass.

Nicole is my cousin, but also my best friend. Just like me, she's a red bone, with nice curves, and a cute face to back it all up. She's been fucking with Terrence trying to make his life a living hell ever since he fucked her and acted like he didn't even know her the next day. His dumb ass doesn't realize that Nicole is the woman that asked him for his number because I was too shy to approach him at the gym, the day that we met. One of my classmates from college steered me to stalk him because she wanted to see his marriage terminated. I was never supposed to sleep with him. I was only supposed to make his wife think that we were having an affair. Coincidentally I did the complete opposite and I ended up being knocked up. Once Nicole witnessed the amount of finances he spent on me and my son she plotted a scheme to

86

get knocked up. When she became an intern at the hospital where Terrence works, she thought that her scandal would be a cake walk.

Her plan backfired on her because he hasn't showed her any interest since they slept together. I'm not mad because she slept with him. He's just another man with a big dick and money. I couldn't care less who he screwed because I'm straight. I don't have to work another day in my life. My paycheck runs around the house everyday rambling through everything that catches his eye. Terrence Donnell Johnson Jr. And since his sorry ass father thinks that he's just going to neglect him and ride off in the sunset with his wife while dripping her in diamonds, Prada, and Chanel, he has another thing coming. I'm going to make his life a living hell.

It's time for Terrence to suffer the consequences for all his hidden secrets. See Terrence has hurt so many women that it's pathetic. Now he's about to pay for it, because what goes around comes around. And that's the damn truth. I'm going to destroy Terrence's marriage if it's the last thing that I do.

14

ALEXIS

Upon pulling up to the home that Terrence and I shared together, I noticed a black Bentley Coupe in the driveway. *His ass must be crazy if he thinks that he's going to have another woman up in there* I thought to myself, as I parked my Rover. *"Better yet I am gon' kill his ass if he has another woman in our bed."* I mumbled to myself as I walked in a quick pace up to the house. I went barreling into the house and Terrence was walking up the staircase. He turned around with an alarmed expression on his face.

"Damn you scared me" He said.

"Sorry" I walked over closer to the staircase and sat down on the first step. I positioned myself sideways. "Whose car is outside?" I quizzed.

"It's yours" He told me as he sat down on a step a few steps up from where I was sitting. He looked distressed. It was hard to believe that he'd washed his face, or even brushed his teeth since I last saw him.

I was appalled. "My car?"

"Yeh, it's your anniversary present"

"How come you didn't tell me anything about it?"

"Because you didn't give me the chance too, you act like you hate me now" He spieled.

I started expressing myself with my hands "I don't hate you Terrence; I hate the way you hurt me."

"It was never my intention to hurt you"

I looked perplexed. "How did you think that sleeping around with other women would make me feel?"

"To be honest" Terrence hung his head down towards his lap. He paused as if he couldn't believe what he was about to say. "I never thought that you would find out"

I became a little perturbed and the look on my face was a very serious one. "So if I would have never found out you would have always slept around on me?"

Terrence grew uncomfortable. "You don't want to know the answer to that question"

I stood up from the steps and walked to the front door in a pissed off kind of mood. Terrence rushed down the steps. "Baby hold up" He said.

I stopped and turned around "Why is it that whenever a man has a good woman at home, he still has to go out and search for something else."

"You'll never understand the answer to that question, because you are not a man and you don't think like one"

"What am I not woman enough for you?"

"It's not about you, I don't know why I cheat, I just do and it's not something I'm proud of"

"You don't know? Well you should've figured that out before you asked me to marry you."

"Baby I'm sorry and I know that I can change, just don't give up on me" He grabbed my hand and said. "I will go to counseling, I will get help. Whatever you want... just tell me want you want. I want us to work. I want to fix this."

As I walked around the house Terrence followed closely behind me. I noticed that the house was filthy. There were dishes in the sink, dirty laundry, broken glass on the floor in the living room, and the food that I cooked nearly three weeks ago; was still in the refrigerator.

"How did the house get so filthy?"

"You haven't been here to clean it." He said gently.

"What's wrong with your hands?"

"I haven't been in the mood to do anything lately"

"Why is that?'

"Don't you see how miserable I am without you?

"Well if you make your bed hard you have to lay in it."

"Well I know that you didn't come by here because you are moving back in. So why are you here?"

"Your mother called me this morning and asked why I wasn't; at your father's funeral. Why didn't you tell me that your dad had passed away?"

"How come you don't want to come back home?"

"Don't change the subject and besides it's not that simple"

"It is simple all you have to do is quit worrying about what everyone will have to say and move back home."

"I don't want to talk about that right now I came here to see how you are doing. And from the looks of things you're not doing to good" I said as I walked into the guest room.

"My life is a mess right now and I need you" Terrence said while sounding as if he was about to break down and cry. To prevent me from witnessing him sob, he walked out of the room. After he'd composed himself he walked back into the room and asked.

"Why want you just stay the night?"

"And then where do we go from there?"

"I don't know but we have to start somewhere" He pulled the rope necklace that he wore around his neck, from under his t-shirt and unhooked it. He slid my wedding ring from it. "This is a start" He grabbed my hand and placed my wedding ring on my finger.

I admired my ring for a moment. "Terrence I don't want what happened the day after our anniversary to be a cycle, my heart can't take it…it just can't take it."

"I'm asking you to give me this one chance, and I promise that I won't hurt you again."

"Promise me that this is not going to be us, promise me that we're not going to be a couple that breaks up and makes up over and over again, because I don't want to live my life that way."

"Baby trust me, when you walked out on me, it felt like my whole world was turned upside down. I thought that you would never speak to me again...be near me again...I even thought about how another man could have the opportunity to steal your heart. That thought crushed me into a million little pieces. So if you give me the chance to prove to you that I can be the man that you deserve I know that I'm not going to fuck it up."

"I will give you another chance. I will come back home"

Terrence's face lit up. He was happy. He picked me up and squeezed me very tight. "I love you"

"I love you to, now put me down I need to clean this house"

I cleaned the entire house and surprisingly Terrence helped. He had never washed a dish since we'd lived together and it was crazy how something that small made me feel that Terrence was really trying to change. But in the back of my mind I knew that it wouldn't be for long.

15

ALEXIS

When I stepped into my employer I just wanted to turn around and go home and I could not wait until 8:00, so that I could do just that. Finally after a tiresome day of work it was time to go home.

When the clock struck eight, I bolted out of the pharmacy like the speed of lightning. I got into my new Bentley Coupe and flushed the pedal to the floor going an hundred miles an hour. Not because I was in that much of a rush to get home but because I had all of a sudden gotten into a tight.

"Keep going; don't stop at the yellow light "I said to the car slowing down in front of me.

"I cannot hold this any longer I feel like I'm about to explode" I mumbled as I drove around the Honda accord. Hoping that there were not any cops around.

I finally made it to my house. I jumped out of my Coupe barely putting it in park. I ran to the front door and forced it open. Terrence had some old Keith Sweat blasting, and the smell of the steak he was cooking hit me dead smack in the face as I spurted by the kitchen. I ran up the stairs and into the bathroom.

"Are you alright baby?" Terrence asked.

"I'm fine. I'm just in a tight" I said loud enough so that he could hear me.

"Well there's a hot bath ready for you in the bathroom" He informed me.

"Okay"

When I made it to the bathroom I was almost nude because I was stripping off my clothes while jogging up the staircase. I tinkled and then walked into our bedroom so that I could grab a night gown. After I gathered my nighties and walked back into the bathroom to enjoy the warm water that Terrence prepared for me in the Jacuzzi, he was stepping in, and was eagerly anticipating my company.

"Damn you sexy" Terrence said as I stepped over into the jacuzzi.

'Thanks" I said in a flabbergast way because I hadn't heard him compliment my physique in years.

He handed me a glass of wine and we both sipped away. "I missed you today" Terrence told me.

"I missed you to" I replied almost choking from the wine. *What in the hell has gotten into him* I thought.

"What's wrong?"

"I'm just shocked. You've never told me that you missed me" I smiled. "Who are you? And what have you done with my husband?"

"This is the new Terrence that loves and respects his wife" Terrence started to sing along with Keith sweat. *"I want to tease you, I want to freak you, I want to show you that I need you, I want you to holler when you want me to stop and who can love you like me nobody, nobody baby"*

I laughed because Terrence could do a lot of things but singing was not one of them.

"What's so funny?"

"Your singing"

"What's wrong with it?" He asked while laughing.

"You just need to let Keith sing it, that's all" I teased.

We talked, kissed, and laughed for about 30 minutes in the Jacuzzi. Afterwards we sat at the table in our bedroom and ate Steak and potatoes.

"Are you going to be my desert tonight baby?"

"Terrence I'm still not ready to have sex"

The old Terrence QUICKLY returned.

"How in the hell do you expect our marriage to work, if we're not having sex?"

"I did not say that I don't ever want to have sex again. I'm saying I'm just not ready right now."

"Have you forgotten how long it's been since we've had sex? I'm a man I have needs"

"Well you should have thought about all that before you cheated"

"You haven't got passed that yet? How are we ever going to move forward if you don't forgive me for it?"

"I have forgiven you but I haven't moved passed it"

"You know what; I'm going to go out for a drink." Terrence said looking angry as he dismissed himself from the table. He walked in a fast pace towards the walk-in closet.

"What's wrong with you?"

"How do you expect me not to step out on you again if you won't have sex with me? Terrence asked as he snatched a pair of jeans out of the closet.

"I'm sorry" I said feeling like I had done something wrong.

"Sorry. Is that all you can say" He feuded. He walked over to the bed and forced his leg down the pair of jeans. Once he was dressed he told me "I'll be back later on tonight I need to get out of this house"

"Baby wait, please---let's just talk about this."

"What is it to talk about it? You've made it very clear that you don't want to have sex with me. If I were you I wouldn't wait up"

Within a matter of seconds he was hastening down the stairs while I tailgated behind him begging him not to leave. He slammed the front door. I opened it, and he was already reversing out of the driveway. I waived my hand in an effort to flag him down. He ignored me. His tires screeched as he drove away leaving me standing there dressed in my robe looking like a fool. I shut the door, twisted the lock, turn around and lean my back up against the door. I slid down the door effortlessly until I ended up sitting on the hardwood floor in our foyer. I cried, like always as I shouted. "Why does he always have to be so damn inconsiderate?"

16

TERRENCE

Well you can't say I didn't try, because I did. How long does Alexis think that I can go without tapping nothing? I'm a man. So I'm going to do what any normal man would do. I'm looking through the contacts in my mobile for the first woman that I know I can call and easily get in her panties with no questions asked and no strings attached. Monique. Monique is a sexy, and might I add single school teacher. Smooth Chocolate skin, nice toned butt, a set of 32 D's and a smile that would lift your spirits on one of your worst days. She jumps at the chance of getting her freak on, every chance she gets. She is so busy all the time that she doesn't get any on the regular. So of course she'll accept my invitation in giving her some of this Grade A dick.

A week ago I got my number changed because Alexis complained every time that my phone rang saying shit like *it's probably your bitch that's why you don't want to answer the phone*. So she probably will not recognize my number when it appears on her caller Id.

"Hello" She answers in her sweet soft sexy voice.

"Whatcha' doing sexy? I ask her.

"Who is this?" She asks sounding upset

"You don't recognize my voice?"

"If I did I wouldn't ask who you are"

"This is Terrence"

"Hey baby" She says.

I notice the instant change in her tone.

"You want some company?"

"Sure, why not"

"I'll be there in fifteen you know how I want you to be when I get there"

"I'll be waiting on you daddy" She says.

I arrive to Monique's house. Put my car in park and hit the alarm button as I shut the door. I walk up to the tower and take the elevator up to the fifth floor. I rang the doorbell. Monique opens the door and she is just the way I like her: dressed in nothing but a thong. She wastes no time pulling at my pants. She throws me down to her leather sofa. Pulls out my dick and gets straight to it. I get my first nut in thirty seconds. I pick Monique up and carry her into her bedroom; I toss her onto her bed and rip her thong apart. Then I begin to eat her pussy like it's a plate of my favorite lasagna in front of me. She begs for me to stop.

"You gotta' stop I'm about to cum" She moans pushing my head away from her vagina" Her resistance is turning me on so I nibble more and flick my tongue back and forth on her clique. "I'm about to cum" She moans...and moans holding my head tightly while her legs tremble.

Just when I know she's about to cum I release my tongue from her vagina and glide my dick between her walls... she cums instantly. Her orgasm glistens on my manhood.

"Oh I've missed your good dick" She tells me throwing her pussy back to me.

"Oh this shit so good!" I tell her trying not to cum

"Don't cum" She tells me.

It's too much I can't hold back so I snatch my dick out and explode all over her naked beautiful body. "Sorry it's been a while" I say. I lay on top of her for a minute before I get up and plant a kiss on her forehead. I clean myself up and later we lay naked in the bed and talk about how life has been treating us. I inform her of the things that are going on in my marriage. Unlike most women Monique understands that there is nothing more to us than a casual fuck every now and then. She and I have been screwing around for about ten years now, every since my last marriage. She doesn't expect me to call her every day, spend the night with her or anything in between. She knows that at the end of the day I have to go back home to wife. And I tip my hat off to her for that. It needs to be more women like her. A few hours have passed and it's time for me to head back home.

"Thanks for tonight" Monique tells me as she walks me to the door. She sighs "I needed that"

"Take care" I say to her.

Do I feel guilty about stepping out on my wife? Hell nah! Because what one woman won't do another woman will. Lately I've been trying to do everything that I can to make this marriage work, but the way I see it is she's been accusing me of fucking around on her anyway, so I may as well do it. It's not my fault she couldn't move forward. How long did she think I was going to keep doing things her way? I tried it and it didn't work. Women throw themselves at me all the time and I'm not the type of guy that misses a catch. I'm addicted to pussy, cougar pussy and young pussy as long as they are over the age of eighteen, middle aged pussy, and there is absolutely nothing like new pussy. Unless the new pussy turns out to be a mentally disturbed, bitter ass woman like Nicole.

Eating pussy is my weakness. I love doing it, almost as much I love receiving it. I love it when a woman is submissive and isn't afraid to talk dirty to me and tell me what she wants.

Nibble it some may say. Others may like for you to suckle the lining of the pussy; others might like for you to finger fuck the pussy and tongue fuck the pussy all at the same time. No matter what her desire is I'm the man for the job. I've been loving pussy every since I got my first piece of ass. And that's been over two decades ago. I'm getting older and I have slowed down at a lot of things but when it comes down to digging in some pussy I haven't slowed down one bit. Back in my younger days, the women use to call me *Dick 'Em Down Good* because that's exactly what I do. I dicks 'em down good! When I'm inside of a woman my mission is making sure that I give her the best dick she's ever had. And most women tell me, I have the energy in the bedroom of an eighteen year old man. Preferably I'd love for it to be wife, that I'm physically pleasing but if I can't have her I have no problem blessing another woman with the many talents that I can possess with my tongue and my manhood.

I know you're probably saying I should have learned my lesson after what happened with Nicole. Well Nicole has calmed down lately. After she burst out my window at my house I guess she figured she'd done enough. She told Alexis about us and caused a little damage. But she didn't destroy us as she had hoped. So I guess she's given up. I really don't know what made her stop harassing me but I'm glad she did.

All I'm going to hear for the rest of the night is how rude it was that I stormed out. I'm just going to pretend to listen for a few minutes and act like I'm sorry, she'll be pissed, but like always, I'll pick her up a Gucci bag or something expensive and she'll forget all about it.

Before I head back home I'm going to stop by a sports bar and have a few cold ones. That should help clear my head.

17

ALEXIS

Damn I should have just given him some instead of trying to play hard to get. As much as I hated to admit it Terrence was right, how were we ever going to move on if I always brought up the past?

Besides, between me and you I wanted some of his good dick anyway. I greeted him at the door once he finally made it back home after being gone for hours. He smelled like a walking bottle of Bud Light. I was nude and very horny when he stepped through the door.

"Let's make a baby" I told Terrence while stripping him down.

"What has gotten into you?"

"Nothing I just want to make love to you I said as I forced him to the stairs.

We didn't even make it to the bedroom because there I was riding Terrence's dick like a cow girl, right there on our staircase. Mmmm that dick was good that day. As soon as I sat down on it, my pussy juices started overflowing. I was already having an orgasm.

"Damn girl that pussy sho' is nice and juicy down there." Terrence said coaching me to ride his dick harder. "Turn on over and let me see that thing from the back." Terrence and I stood up. I bent down with my ass sticking straight up in the air, Terrence stood right behind me and eased the head of his dick in my pussy.

"Uhhh Terrence" I moaned. "Go deeper"
Terrence slapped me on the ass and penetrated all nine inches, quicker and deeper. For a moment I thought I was in heaven. He knew exactly how to please me. The sound of Terrence's balls slapping up against my ass made me cum over- and over- and over again.

"Damn that was good" Terrence said after we were done.

"Your mama should have named you Campbell soup because your sex is Mmm Mmm Good" I chuckled.

"I know that I'm going to sleep good tonight, I feel like a million bucks now." Terrence said while carrying me up to our bedroom.

We lay in bed snuggled close, and for the first time in years, I was happy. I felt like there was hope for our marriage, and that we were going to fix it together.

After Terrence was sound asleep I went into the kitchen to fix me a glass of water. I finished my water and picked up Terrence's clothes off the floor. I noticed that he did not have on the same color boxer briefs that he wore when he left the house. *I know that I 'm not crazy* I thought to myself *"his ass had on some blue boxer briefs when he left the house"* I muttered. Just as I was saying that, I heard a vibration coming from his pant pockets and it was his cell phone. He had 1 new text message. The message said. ***I really enjoyed you tonight; I just can't get you off of my mind. No one has ever eaten my pussy like you. I can't understand why your wife would turn you down. Thanks. TTYL…***

Talk about Kharma, because reading that made me feel queasy and sick to my stomach I covered my mouth with my hand ran into the bathroom and there I was vomiting for the next 30 minutes. Finding out that my husband had just given another woman oral sex not even an hour before having sex with me, turned my stomach upside down. Finally I walked upstairs into bedroom.

"Wake your ass up" I told Terrence while slapping him in his head.

"Baby what's wrong?'

"All that talk about how you're not gon' cheat on me no more, you're going to change and do right by me was all bullshit"

"I have changed" Terrence said looking as though he was wondering where I was going with what I'd just said to him.

"Oh you've changed? Well explain this" I yelled at Terrence while slamming his cell phone down into his face.

"What in the hell are you doing going through my cell phone?" He asked me as he sat up in the bed.

"What is another woman doing telling you how good you made her feel tonight?"

"If you wouldn't have been going through my phone you wouldn't have to walk around with your feelings hurt."

"No, I wouldn't be hurt if you would consider my feelings sometimes instead of only caring about your on damn self." I screamed at Terrence while punching him as hard as I could in the face.

"Stop hitting me" Terrence demanded.

"Stop cheating on me and we wouldn't have to go through this" I cried out.

"Calm down Alexis" Terrence said while he grabbed my arms to keep me from hitting him" While restraining me, he eased up from the bed. "Chill out" He insisted as he released his handgrip and pushed me onto the bed.

"Get out" I screamed with tears running down my cheeks as I hopped off the bed and paced over to the chest drawer.

"Where am I going to go?"

"I don't know, but this time I am not leaving; YOU ARE" I started throwing all of Terrence's clothes out of the drawer. "Go and stay with all the women you keep messing around with"

"I'm not going anywhere"

"Oh you're not going to leave?" I asked as I rushed over to the night stand, and grabbed Terrence's nine millimeter.

"Alexis what are you doing?"

106

"I'm going to shoot your ass if you don't get out of here?"

"Just put that thing down before you do something you will regret' Terrence said looking like he was about to pee in his pants." He was dressed in only his boxer briefs

"Get out "I yelled as I put my finger on the trigger.

"I'm leaving" Terrence said as he hurriedly put on his clothes.

"Nowwwww" I demanded. Terrence was barefoot as he jolted down the stairs. "I hate you" I screamed.

What kind of person had I become, pulling out a gun? I had never even touched a gun before, let alone pointed it at someone. I needed some guidance and I found myself on my knees praying that night. *Lord, please give me the strength to leave Terrence alone. Give me the strength to be strong and move on with my life. Please give me the courage to walk from this marriage.*

I was tired of all the pain and constant betrayal.

Once I calmed down I logged onto the computer, and noticed that Terrence did not log out of his email account. And because of the fact that I had every reason not to trust his ass- I read all of his emails. Most of them were all junk mail but the one that caught my eye was a message from a woman named Janice. She was highly upset with Terrence because in the email she was cursing him out. *You know good ass low down and dirty bastard, how can you change your number and not bother to give me*

107

your new number. If I have to continue chasing you down to get some money I am going to go down to child support enforcement and take out child support.

Child support I know his ass hasn't had a baby on me I mumbled to myself. I then logged onto Verizonwireless.com and hacked into Terrence's account. I called all the numbers that he'd called at 2 and 3 o'clock in the morning. Most of them were women as I suspected. After calling majority of them, I finally dialed Janice's number. The first time I called her I got her voice mail. *Hi, you've reached your girl Janice sorry that I'm unable to answer your call but if you would, please leave me a quick and detailed message and I'll get back with you at my earliest convenience.*

So I continued to call her for nearly two hours. Finally she answered.

"Hello"

"Hello Janice"

"Hi…who's this?"

"This is Terrence's wife"

"And I am the mother of his child." She snapped back.

"Terrence does not have a child you're just after his money."

"Look as long as Terrence signed the birth certificate, I don't give a damn what lies he tells you"

"If Terrence had a child I would know it."

"You are such a dumb broid, where do you think Terrence is on the nights that he's not at home with you?"

"When I see you, I'm going to kick your ass" I shouted at her.

"Well you don't have to wait until then, I'll come to you. Should I come to your house or do you want me to come to your job? because it does not matter to me." She said angrily.

"Bitch you don't know where I live"

"Know where you live" She giggled. "I've been inside of your house." Janice went on and on describing every inch of my house. And then she went on to say. "You think you got yourself something. Terrence ain't shit. So what you married to him, because we all get his money. You were just the one stupid enough to fall for his game."

She hung up the phone leaving me with a dial tone and unanswered questions.I felt like the dumbest woman walking the face of the earth, because all that time I had been telling myself that Terrence did not take care of any of the women that he'd cheated with. And to find out that he did made me feel real foolish.

I couldn't fall asleep because I had too much on my mind and I needed answers to the thousands of questions float-ing around in my head. Although Terrence and I had ended the night on a bad note I called him to clear my mind from the many things that were weighing heavy on my heart.

"I read your email from Janice and I know that you are the father of her child and I also know that she's been in our house." I said with the voice of a person that was heartbroken.

"I don't have a baby, that woman is lying"

"It's not your baby" I asked.

"No I've never had sex with that woman, she came onto me and after I turned her down, she's been stalking me. I would never hurt you like that" He said convincingly. "I would never get another woman pregnant" I have more respect for you than that"

Even though I had spoken to Janice and she described my house to a tee. I still sided with my husband. I had begun to let money, and good sex control my decisions.

It was around this time that I first noticed that I was not the same person anymore. I was losing weight, my hair was falling out, and I was crying more than I was smiling. I would look in the mirror and I would see Alexis, but I didn't feel like Alexis. Alexis had left years ago. I was drowning in my own misery, and no matter how hard I tried to paddle above the water, I could never seem to stay afloat.

18

TERRENCE

I just hung up the phone with Alexis and I'm lying in a king size bed at the Westin hotel with my mobile in my hand, staring at the ceiling in deep thought.

Not that I want to be here alone, it's more like I don't have a choice. Monique's text, had already put my ass in hot water, and, Janice's email only added fuel to the fire. I know that I fuck up a lot, but in essence I truly do love Alexis. She's always told me that she'll rather be hurt by the truth than hurt by a lie any day. I can't say that I believe that. And that's exactly why I refuse to tell her that I did fuck Janice, and my blood is flowing through her child's veins. I really do want to come clean about everything but I mean at this point, what am I supposed to say? *I'm sorry baby.....I've been lying to you this whole time, I did fuck Janice and I have a two year old son with her.* Skeletons do come out of the closet, but I'm going to try my best to keep her from finding out that

Janice is telling the truth. Even if that means I have to start back screwing around with Janice, just to do so. That's basically the only reason that she's been tripping so hard lately because I've been giving her the cold shoulder. If it was left up to her we would fuck on an everyday basis. I'm not able to do it like that anymore. Tonight, I tried to make love to my wife, and after she turned me down I ended up with Monique, just because I needed a piece of ass. Then I went home, and my wife, went straight to work on me. I don't understand how I did it. I guess it was the Bud Light. I'm in my forties and even though I can keep going and going like an energizer bunny, having sex with two different women, in the same night back to back, is a bit much.

Counseling may be the route to go, for me, because if I don't get some help I may end up losing the most important person in my life. She's the best I ever had, hands down. Only a fool wouldn't commit to her. I guess that makes me a fool. I don't know what's wrong with me, I think it's because I have some issues when it comes to putting my trust in a woman, and it started when I was a young boy.

I can recall plenty of nights when my mother would have different guys, over while my dad was at work breaking his back to take care of her. This was a ritual for her, until she got pregnant with Terry and was unsure if whether or not my dad was his father. We lived in a small town in Missouri, and because my mother had gained herself a reputation and was known around town for her promiscuous behavior, word traveled fast that it was a possibility that my mother wasn't carrying my pops child. Pops heard the rumors and asked if whether or not they were true. Surprisingly she admitted that she'd been cheating and my pops moved out. This didn't last long at all because my pops loved my mother unconditionally, flaws and all. He moved back in. I vaguely remember the conversation they had when he came back home. But I do remember him stating that he didn't care if my brother Terry was his or not, because he was going to raise him like he was his flesh and blood either way. He was a hellova' man, because I know that I can never be, the man that will be able to accept my wife cheating on me and getting pregnant by another man. However, things started to change around the house, my mother started to appreciate my dad more and all of the sneaking around behind his back ceased. But look what had to happen for it to stop. For a long time I despised her, and in my eyes she was a whore. As I got older I forgave her, and we became closer. But because of the relationship I had with my mother and the relationship that I shared with my first love, whom dumped me for absolutely no reason has precluded my ability to commit myself 100%. Those scars have never healed and I've never been able to give my whole heart to Alexis or any other woman.

I really do love my wife but I've done so much trifling shit to her, that I wouldn't be surprised if she's gone for good. If she ever finds out that I've been lying to her this whole time it's going to take some counseling, God, and a miracle to save my marriage.

19

JANICE

That bitch has some nerve calling my damn phone; she needs to check that trifling husband of hers. Because whether he or she likes it or not my child does exist and it isn't a damn thing that either of them can do about it.

I've been up all day and mostly all night with a sick child, because my child has the sniffles, along with a runny nose, and runny eyes. The last thing that I'm worried about is Terrence and his dumb ass wife. When I'm done with the two of them, the money that they blow on shopping sprees and buying luxury cars is going to have to come to an end. I'm going to get an attorney and get every penny my son deserves.

I finally was able to get T.J. to fall asleep. I cleaned the house, folded the clothes that's been in the dryer since yesterday, and took me a long hot shower. Afterwards I popped me a bag of popcorn and watched re-runs of Martin and Living Single. Shortly after that I'd fallen as leep but was awoken by an unexpected knock on the door. I quickly put on my robe and rushed to the door.

"Who is it?"

"Terrence"

"What do you want Terrence?"

"Open the damn door"

I cracked open the door. "What?" I asked. Terrence pushed open the door and walked in. "Why in the hell did you call my wife?"

"I didn't call your wife. Your wife called me"

"I don't give a damn who called who. Why did you tell her about T.J.?"

"Because I wanted to"

"We have a deal. You are to never mention TJ to anyone especially not my wife" He said angrily.

"That's what you wanted. I agreed to it as long as you took care of your responsibility. But I haven't seen you in a month. It's been almost a month since you gave me a dime for T.J."

"That's because every time I turn around I'm giving you thousands of dollars. I told you the last time that I talked to you, if TJ needs anything, tell me what he needs and I'll go out and buy it. I'm not going to continue giving you money and every time I see my son he looks like a throwed away child."

"Kiss my ass"

"Cancel that, I told you that's what has me in this situation in the first place."

"Whatever you know you miss this. You know you want this pussy"

"See that's the problem. That's why you been tripping so hard lately, because I refuse to sleep with you."

T.J. starts crying and I walk out of the living room
and return with him in my arms.

"What's wrong with him" Terrence asks as if he's
concerned.

"He has a cold"

"Has he seen a pediatrician?"

"No he hasn't"

"And why is that?"

"Because I don't have any transportation"

"See that's the shit I'm talking about, as much
money that you get from me you could have bought a car
by now, but you don't have anything to show for it. What
in the hell do you do with the money? I need to know.
Look at this damn place. I'm going to tell Alexis the truth
about TJ and then I'm going to get sole custody of my
son."

"Fuck you. As long as I'm living you will never
have my son around that bitch."

"Is that a threat?"

"Consider it a promise; I'll kill you and her before
I watch the two of you raise my child."

"You sound just like the stupid ass woman that
you are" Terrence tries to walk to the door with TJ in his
arms.

"Where do you think that you are going with my
child?"

"He's my child to"

"Now you want to claim him as your son"

"Look he needs to see a doctor"

"You are a doctor"

"I'm a gynecologist, not a pediatrician"

"And your point"

"Look he needs to be seen okay"

"You want be taking him"

"For once will you put him first?"

"I am and he is not going anywhere with you"

"Okay fine, I'm going to go down the street to the CVS and get him some Tylenol." He handed me TJ and left the house.

Terrence returned about twenty minutes later with the medicine. He gave TJ his dosage and rocked him to sleep. Afterwards he put him in his bed. I was standing in the bedroom door watching.

"I'm sorry Terrence" I told him as I walked inside the room.

"For what?"

"The way I've been acting lately"

"You need to start thinking about TJ instead of always thinking about yourself and what you want.

"I know it's just hard raising a child alone, and sometimes I get frustrated. We use to talk on the phone, we use to make love, and we use to do a lot of things. But now I barely get a phone call."

"It's not good for us to carry on like we are a family; I don't want to complicate things any more than they already are."

"Can we make love just this one time? I miss it"

"That's not a good idea. We need to keep things strictly about TJ."

I unravel my robe. "Please just one last time"

"No. That's over."

"I do not believe that. I said pulling at Terrence's belt buckle."

"What kind of mother are you? Attempting to have sex with me with our son lying right here."

"Get out of my house"

"This is the government's house not yours"

"Fuck you"

He giggles. "I know you want to" He kisses TJ on the cheek. "See you in court soon"

"I'm not worried about that because I know how to fix you. You better hope you get to your wife before I do"

20

ALEXIS

The next day, was a Saturday and I would have rather been home in my bed. But because our annual inventory was scheduled for that following Monday instead I was at work. Jody was tidying up things around the store and I was standing at the customer counter glancing at my weekly reports so that when it was time to get off I could fax them to the corporate office without having to stay over a minute later. Pam my assistant was in the stock room making sure that everything was in the proper codification for our annual inventory.

Work was wearisome for me majority of the time, especially on days that I could count the number of customers that came into the store literally on one hand. That's why I was happy when the first customer since around 12 o'clock that morning walked up to the counter.

"Hello how are you doing today… and what can I do for you?"

Her attire was a skin tight knee length dress that looked like it had been painted on her. It was too small for her big ass. Long weave hung down her back that looked like it had been in her head for at least ten years. And the knock off purse that she was carrying, signaled that she was trying to portray herself as someone that she wasn't. Surely she was not the type of woman I pictured as being Terrence's type. He always quoted. *I don't like ghetto women; I like women of sophistication and class.* Maybe he just liked to hear himself talk, because clearly she did not define classy. In my opinion she was just a redbone with a big ass.

"I'm doing well. I'm here to pick up a prescription for my son Terrence Donnell Johnson Jr."

Without grasping what she'd said at first hand, I asked "what's his birthday?" I paused. "What did you say his name was again?"

"Yeh.....you heard me right, Terrence Donnell Johnson Jr."

"Look Helfa, I don't know what type of games you playing but my husband has already told me all about you, I know that you just a hood rat bitch looking for a way to come up and you think that my husband is your way out of the ghetto- but guess what I don't believe a damn thing that you're saying."

"Do you think that I care whether or not you believe me? Because let me tell you one thing, those checks that I receive every month is all I care about"

"Look just get your ghetto ass out of my eyesight before shit gets really ugly"

"You should have been keeping your husband satisfied and maybe…just maybe, he wouldn't have been digging in my ghetto ass pussy bitch. Where do you think he is all those nights that he's not with you….at work? I know that you are not that naïve. It must be lonely in that big beautiful house all alone? Yeh, I been in your house, in your bed, with your husband. You should really change the wall coloring in the kitchen that pea green doesn't do anything for the countertops. Regardless of what you think your man is my baby daddy. See this is the difference between me and you. I know that Terrence isn't shit. That's why I got knocked up. Because with or without him I'm going to be paid….Tootles" She said waving her hand goodbye.

The entire time that she was standing there bragging about how she'd been fucking my man and had a baby by him. I stood there in shock and didn't utter one word. The shit was crazy because rather that plan to leave Terrence for good the only thing that I was thinking about was if she was in fact telling the truth how was the baby going to fit into our lives because I knew that Terrence was going to linger around the store and pop up at Lisa's house claiming that he'd changed and like always I was going to take him back.

"Bitch" I shouted before Jody blocked me from hurdling over the customer counter.

"Let that bitch go, she ain't gon' do shit" Janice chimed in.

"She isn't worth you losing your job" Jody insisted trying his best to restrain me.

"Fuck this job…let me go" I screamed.

"Girl you can go to jail"

"Fuck that! If she's bad enough to come to my job with this bullshit she needs to be bad enough to take an ass whipping."

"Bitch please, bring it on"

I clawed Jody, biting and kicking, struggling to break free. But Jody had a grip on me so tight that it was difficult for me to distance myself away from him.

All the commotion caused an enormous scene. That's why I wasn't shocked when Pam came barging out to the floor.

"What's going on out here" She puzzled.

Jody separated from me. "Guurrlll…I need my job" He explained.

"This woman is trying to fight me sir" Janice protested, while grinning because of the fact that she knew that she'd put my job on the line.

"She's lying. Look there is an explanation for all of this" I explained.

"I hope it is….Mrs. Johnson you are the store manager and you're supposed to set an example for your staff. As assistant manager it's my responsibility to be sure that I put what's best for the store first, and with that being said, I'm going to have to call corporate office and report this. I don't know what's been going on with you lately but I believe that your letting personal situations interfere with you work ethic. No matter what happened between the two of you, customers are always right, even though sometimes I know that they are not."

"Please don't tell anyone in the corporate office about this, my husband and I may be going through a divorce and I need this job"

I hated to air out my business while Janice was standing there meddling in my misery but I was in a very bad place. A place of desperation, with no way out unless I confessed my many problems, and hoped that they would let me off the hook.

"I'm going to have to ask you to leave mam" Jody informed Janice and he marched her out of the store.

"Customers are always right bitch" She quoted as she walked away.

"I didn't know that you were going through all of that. I think you need to take the rest of the day off. I can handle things." Pam told me.

"Are you sure?"

"Of course! I'm almost done with the inventory, and, we haven't been busy today so I should be able to finish with the paperwork in no time. Go home and get some rest before you have an anxiety attack or something worse."

"Okay" I sighed. "I'll see you next week, call me if you need anything"

The expression on my face showed that I was humiliated because I'd just made myself look like a complete a-hole at my place of employment. I hated the fact that Jody heard the entirety of the argument that I had with Janice because we'd just had a quarrel about Terrence's infidelity weeks earlier. I'm pretty sure he was thinking that I was dumbest woman he'd ever met. Especially when he heard Janice point out the color of my kitchen. I still didn't know if she truly had a baby by my husband. But one thing was for sure, she'd definitely been in our home.

I didn't know who to believe, on one hand there was Terrence telling me that he'd never had sex with the woman, and then on the other hand the chic was telling me that Terrence was the father of her son. I had more than enough reasons not to believe a word that came out of Terrence's mouth, because over the years he had proven to me that he was a habitual liar-But at the same time, Janice could have very much been a gold digger, and I knew that gold diggers flocked to men with money like flies sticking to animals shit.

I gave Terrence the benefit of the doubt by giving him one last chance to come clean about everything, and then maybe we could work things out. But I needed to know the truth first. As I sat in my vehicle outside of my place of employment I dialed his number and slowly exhaled as it hit me that I was about to ask a question, that depending on the answer, my life could be changed forever.

"I have surgery in about three minutes" He said as soon as he answered. "I'll call you back when I'm done"

"We need to talk now" I ordered before he could say another word. "Did you fuck the bitch or not?"

"What bitch?"

"The bitch that's claiming she's got a child by you"

"Look Alexis, I've told you once and now I'm telling you again. No."

"Well Terrence…It's your fault I don't believe a word you say. All you do is lie"

"I'm telling you the truth. I have never touched that woman"

"Well I'm having a hard time figuring out why that bitch would come to my job and ask for a prescription for Terrence Donnell Johnson Jr. if you've never slept with her"

The phone was silent and I heard heavy breathing, as if Terrence was enraged.

"She came to your job?"

"Why would I tell you that if she didn't"

"Whewwwwwww….The woman is obsessed with me. She is crazy as hell."

"Umm-huh… well how come she told me exactly what color the paint is in our kitchen?"

"Babe, I gotta' call you back surgery is about to start"

Click.

The second I hung up the phone with Terrence, after he abruptly ended our conversation, there was a little voice in my head saying take your ass to his job, and stake him out. I don't know why my conscious told me that I should go to his job and sit under the employee parking deck, but that's exactly what I did.

I beelined may way around the traffic and headed straight to his job. I made sure that I parked close enough so that I could see Terrence get into his vehicle but not so close that he would recognize my car. Being that he'd told me that he was going to be in surgery, I planned on being there for majority of the evening. Ten minutes later: what do you know, guess who came drifting into the parking lot? My no good ass husband! What happened to the surgery that he was supposedly scheduled for?

After he'd gotten into his vehicle I followed behind him closely for nearly thirty minutes as I wondered where in the hell he was headed. We ended up in a neighborhood that was similar to the neighborhood I was raised in, which means that it wasn't a pretty sight. Once Terrence had gotten out of the car, I watched as he walked up to the door and knocked. The door opened and he walked inside. The door opened again and Terrence walked out, with a car seat in his possession.

As he was loading the car-seat in the back seat of his car, a woman, who resembled the same woman that came to my job, came out of the apartment carrying a child. She and Terrence were feuding back forth.

"That's what you get...I told you, that I know how to fix your ass. I told you that I was going to tell her everything." She had opened the door to the backseat of the car and was strapping the child in the car seat.

"Yo' ass just mad, because I quit hopping up and damn near breaking a leg every time that you wanted me to"

"Well I told you a long time ago that I would keep quiet as long as you made sure that my pockets were straight"

"Damnet Janice what do you mean I don't give you any money?"

"It's not enough"

"What do you mean it's not enough? Terrence said furiously. He calmed down and asked "What do I have to do make you keep quiet about all of this"

"You can start by buying me a car so that u won't have to haul me around every time that I need to go somewhere, and giving me some dick, every now and then would be nice"

"Get in the car"
There feud ended after that and they both hopped into Terrence's car. All of sudden I snapped, and I don't know who the person was that came out of me, but I was way out of my character. The anger had taken over my actions. I unbuckled my seatbelt and virulently stepped out of my car and eased up to the driver side of Terrence's car.

Nervousness was his expression when I poked him with my finger on the side of his temple and he turned to see that it was me. Fear showed in his eyes but of course he couldn't show that I'd demoralized him.

"Alexis just go home, don't start with any dumb shit"

I struck him in the head a few times. "You been fucking this bitch and lying to me? And you got me out here looking like a fool!"

"Stop fucking hitting me" He insisted, in between punches while he tried to avoid them"

The child in the back seat was crying hysterically and Terrence started the engine of the car. He rolled up his window before me and that's when I shouted. "Oh…so you're just going to disrespect me like this and drive off with this bitch?" I galloped around to the back of the car and sprinted to the passenger door and yanked on the door handle. "Get out of the car bitch" I roared.

Terrence reversed his car and sped off. Quickly I ran to my car and in no time I was dead on his ass ramming my new Coupe in the rear of his Corvette, thinking that this would force him to pull over. Not one time, did I think about the kid that must have been traumatized in the back seat! After I realized that crashing into the back of Terrence's car was not enough to make him maneuver over. I drove around to the side of his car.

"Pull your ass over" I yelled.
He was doing everything in his power to escape. He exceeded the speed of his car to the max. This still did not stop me because I hit the accelerator on my vehicle and we both drove pass the red traffic light. Two cops that were alongside the road pulled us over.

"Fuck" I said banging on the stirring wheel.

We pulled over into the parking lot of a convenience store. Before the cop made it to my driver side window I fished in my purse for my license and pulled my insurance card from out of the glove compartment.

"Mam are you aware that you were speeding?" The officer asked.

"Yeh, I'm aware of it"

"What is the reason that you were driving so fast?"

"I just caught my no good ass husband cheating with that bitch, and not only did he cheat-he got that bitch pregnant!" I vented.

"I need to see your license and registration please?"

I handed the officer my GA driver's license and insurance card. He collected them from me and walked back over to his patrol car. Moments later he stood beside my passenger side window. Before he could begin talking the officer that was standing alongside Terrence's vehicle called him over.

He walked away again but this time he walked over to the patrol officer that was questioning Terrence. They had a discussion before he walked back over to my vehicle.

"Mam, could I get you to step out of the car please?" After a few more questions he said. "I'm sorry mam but I'm afraid that you are under arrest for child cruelty" He put the handcuffs around my wrists and he walked me over to his patrol car, opened the door and I got in the back seat.

Once Terrence saw the officer putting the handcuffs on me, he hurriedly ran over. "Officer don't take her to jail, this is entirely my fault."

He stood there while we drove off and as we rode pass Terrence's car I took a good look at the little boy, who was the spitting image of Terrence and I knew that he was Terrence's son.

I spent the entire weekend in a county jail because I did not receive a bond until the following Monday at 11 o'clock. Terrence posted my bail.

Back in the car that following Monday, as soon as Terrence and I were off of the jail house grounds I lifted my leg up high enough so that I could kick his ass upside the head. I kicked him in the head so hard that his head slammed against the driver side window.

"Bitch what did you do that for?" He shouted after losing his temper.

"Oh I'm a bitch now"

"Well that's what you are acting like"

"I had to spend my entire weekend locked up while you were probably out fucking your baby mama."

"It's not my fault you got locked up you should have not been looking for something you didn't want to find."

After Terrence said that to me, as if he didn't care about my feelings- or the fact that I had just spent the weekend in jail. I jumped on top of him while he was driving and started punching him as hard as I could.

"Alexis stop hitting on me; I can't see we are going to have a wreck."

"I don't give a damn" I screamed at him still fighting. I didn't stop fighting Terrence until I was too tired to keep going, which was when we pulled into our driveway.

"Get your ass out of the car" Terrence told me as he snatched open the passenger side door.

"You should have just told me truth?"

"Look at how you are acting "

"How am I supposed to act, I'm sick and tired of you hurting me."

"Well everything is out in the open now; the baby is mine you are just going to have to figure out a way to deal with it."

"I'm not dealing with shit, I want a divorce!"

"You want a divorce?"

"Yes, I can't do this anymore."

"Look! Let's just think about this."

"What is it to think about?"

"Think about the life that we've built together. I know that I fuck up from time to time but, you are the woman that I love."

"Love will make you think about our marriage before you do things to jeopardize it. Love is just not enough anymore." I said with tears in my eyes again.

"What can I do to make it up to you? I'll do anything"

"The only thing that you can do for me is sign your name on the dotted line when you receive your divorce papers."

21

ALEXIS

I filed for divorce after everything went down. Around that time I started wild'n out with Moesha. I got married so young that I never really got to experience things like going out and partying. Once I became Terrence's wife, he desolated me from everyone that cared anything about me. Being that he was fifteen years older than me, sometimes he treated me like I was his daughter and not his wife. He wouldn't have ever approved the attire that I wore the day that Moesha and I stepped out to the club. I should have just left the house naked, being that I wore as less clothing that I possibly could without it being illegal.

Everybody and they mama was at the spot that night. The parking lot was packed and I could tell that it was nothing but ballers inside the club because of all the Benzes, Rolls Royces, Jaguars and every type of top-of-the-line vehicle that you could think of was parked in

VIP. We hopped out of my car and the valet driver hopped right in. We walked into the club.

The DJ was on point and the crowd was crunk. Lights were flashing and all you could see was booties out, breast perked up, and men acting like animals. All eyes were on Moesha and I, which, was not unusual- because every time that we went out guys would always be trying to hit on us. There were only a handful of cute girls in the club and Moesha and I were in the top 10.

I ended up being by myself that night because Moesha wanted to be up under Suede. Suede was just this aggravating ass guy that latched on her like a tick on a dog as soon as we walked through the door. He was an older sugga daddy and she was hanging around him so that she could get whatever dollar she could out of him. It was 1:30 in the a.m. and I was walking towards the ladies room hoping that I would spot Moesha inside. Because I was ready to leave and guess who I spotted posted up against the wall outside the entrance of the ladies room? Marcus. Looking as fine as ever! I just wanted to walk up to him and tell him *I'm going home with you tonight*. He was wearing a black polo shirt, a pair of denim colored polo jeans, and some all black Air Jordan. I walked pass him and went inside the ladies room.

"I hope that his ass is not still standing out there" I mumbled to myself as I stood around trying to kill time. I waited about ten minutes and I finally walked out of the restroom.

"Hey there sexy" Marcus said while tugging on my arm as I walked by.

I could smell the cologne he was wearing -*Polo Black* by Ralph Lauren.

I turned around and faced him. "Hi" I spoke.

"You were gonna' just walk right pass me without saying anything?" Marcus asked.

"I didn't know if you brought someone with you tonight and I didn't want to get you in any trouble"

"Nooo...I'm by myself. Speaking of that: where is your husband? I can't believe he let you out dressed like that, especially by the way he was acting when I dropped you off at your homegirls house." Marcus was doing his best to talk over the loud music.

"We're not together anymore"

"Since when?"

"Since a week ago"

"So I guess I can take you out now?"

"There you go again"

"I'm serious though, but you'll never know if you don't give me the chance to prove it to you."

"It's too soon for all of that"

"Are you here by yourself?"

"No my girlfriend Moesha is around here some-where"

"You looking good tonight"

"Thanks...I can hardly hear myself think let's go outside." I yelled.

Marcus grabbed my hand and led us out of the club.

Now that we were sitting in Marcus's car, we continued with the conversation.

"So what did he do?"

"He got another woman pregnant"

"Whoa that's fucked up!"

"And trust me, that's just the beginning of the story"

"We have time"

"I really don't want to talk about it right now"

"That's understandable"

"Marcus can I ask you a question"

"What's up?" He reclined the passenger side seat and laid back.

"Why aren't you married?"

"It's a long story"

"We have all the time in the world"

"Look at you, not willing to give me any information about you but yet you're sitting here questioning me" He joked. "I was married to my child's mother we've been divorced now for about a year in a half."

"What happened?" I asked

"Well growing up I moved from foster home to foster home and majority of my life I was made to believe that I wasn't worthy to be loved. All I ever wanted was for someone to love me. I met Chasity when I was 17 years old and she was my first love. Back then I was into the streets and that whole lifestyle. Eventually I got mixed up with the wrong crowd and started selling drugs

135

for King Pen"

"So that's how you know King Pen"

"Yeh"

"Are you still cool with him?"

"Fuck no"

"Why not?"

"Let me get to it!"

"Okay, I'm listening" I said anxiously.

"I was living what I thought was the good life. But it wasn't long before the feds kicked in my door. I had money put up and Chasity was well taken care of. I did 13 years in prison. And she stood by my side. When I got out of prison I turned my life around and I married her. Shortly after we got married she gave birth to our son... and then she started to change. I did everything I could to make our marriage work. I didn't deserve everything that she was putting me through. Finally God gave me the strength to walk away from it. The hardest part for me was not living in the same house as my son."

"When you say she changed...What do you mean changed?

"You know how you women get when you have a good man, you try and take advantage of him...to make a long story short we got divorced and I haven't been with another woman since.

"Do you get to see your son?"

"Sometimes....when his mom wants to go club-bing."

""How could she let a good man like you slip through her fingers?"

"Most women claim that they want a good man and when they get one they run up behind the man that's going upside there head."

"Not all women"

"Yeh, well I don't agree with you on that one."

"So had the feds been watching you are what? How did you get hemned up?"

"That bitch ass nigga King Pen set me up. One of the young cats that use to sell for him got pulled over in a routine traffic stop. The police started putting the heat on his ass and he ratted out King Pen. But King Pen is like mad paid. So he hired this top of the line lawyer because the word on the street was that the lawyer was best friends with a couple of high power motherfuckers that could get him off the hook. And that's what they did, they got King Pen off the hook but in order to do that they pinned me for everything. Making it look like I was a major supplier for the drug trafficking in more than twenty states. His ass thought that he was being a good sumeritan because he got my time down to thirteen years served and 15 years on parole"

"I knew that it was something sneaky and grimy about him"

"Hell yeh that motherfucker is grimy as hell, your friend better be careful, because before he does a day in jail he'll drag her down first. That motherfucker has a lot of secrets"

"Do you think that I should tell her?"

"That's up to you, but if you do tell her, your life is going to be in danger, if she questions him about it"

"That's something I'm going to have to sleep on. I love Lisa like she's my sister, but I don't want to put myself in danger"

"I don't want you to put yourself in danger either....but hey it's getting late. We oughta' go back in? Your girl is probably thinking that you've left her"

"Yeh we probably should"

In the time that it took Marcus and I to walk back inside the club we ran into Christopher. Christopher was Terrence's good friend and the district manager of the company that I worked for. We both said hello to each other. He was looking confused. So I knew that it wouldn't be long before he would be calling Terrence to question him. Christopher was just nosey like that. I distanced myself from Marcus that instant.

Now back in the club I was a nervous wreck because I was sure that Christopher had called Terrence and spilled the beans. Although Terrence and I were separated, I didn't want Terrence to come to the club and flip out. Because that's exactly what he was going to do once he found out. I searched for Moesha for nearly an hour before I found her. As usual she was so drunk that she could barely stand up straight.

"Girl I've been looking for you, for damn near an hour, I'm ready to go"

"Why are you ready to leave? This club is what's up"

"Girl we've gotta' go, I have a strange feeling that Terrence is going to pop up here and show his ass"

"What makes you think that?"

138

"I'll tell you in the car, let's get out of here"

I grabbed Moesha by the arm and we headed out of the club moving as quickly as we could. I didn't have the time or the patience to wait for the driver and luckily I brought my spare key. I ambled to the VIP parking section. There was no sign of Terrence and I was relieved.

"Where in the hell is my car" I said out loud.

"I...........don't know" Moesha remarked with a slurred speech"

I circled around the VIP area for at least twenty minutes before my mobile started to ring. The number was private but I answered anyway.

"Hello"

"Your car is not there anymore" Terrence chuckled.

"What do you mean?"

"I'm sitting here looking at you, while you search for your car" He flashed his lights at me.

"Terrence what have you done with my car"

"Wrong…What have I done with my car? I had it towed to my home. Since you want to be up in the club looking like a damn ho and cuddle up with another man, then you go ahead but you're not going to have anything that belongs to me."

"I wasn't hugged up with anyone"

"Well that's not what Christopher told me"

"Christopher is lying"

"I'm through with this conversation Alexis, just like I'm through with this marriage"

"Terrence I need my car how am I supposed to get to work"

"Work… what do you mean work? I got you that job and I'll make damn sure that you get fired."

"Terrence pleeeassse, don't do this to me"

"Goodbye Alexis"

He drove off. And there Moesha and I were standing in front of the club with no vehicle and no way home.

22

TERRENCE

Christopher wouldn't lie to me, she probably was standing outside of the club all booed up with another man. She didn't have any business being out there anyway, half damn naked. I don't know what has gotten into her, because she's definitely not the woman I married. I'm going to give her ass what she wants. She wants a divorce, so that's what I'm going to give her. I hope she knows that she's walking away from this marriage with exactly what she walked into it with, nothing.

I drove off, leaving her in the parking lot stranded. She's crazy as hell if she thinks for one second that she's just going to use me. Before she rides around town with another man in the car that I bought, I'll rather watch her ass catch the bus.

I'm covering up my heartache very well at the moment because deep down inside I really do love her and I'm trying to tell myself to relax and don't sweat it because women come a dime a dozen. I've been putting her ass on a pedestal like she's perfect, and here she is hanging out in clubs dressed like a damn skank. And because of that, I'm going to be very vengeful. I know that I've done plenty of shit, but I'm a man, and I can do that. A woman is to do what men say they are not supposed to do as we do. I feel like I've been violated, humiliated, and disrespected. How could she be hugged up with another man only a week after our split?

But that's okay because as soon as I walk into my home, anything that belongs to her I'm going to load it in my car and drive over to Lisa's house and toss it into the front yard. And I don't give a damn what happens to it.

Later, I drive over to Lisa's house so that I could do as I plan, and that's, to throw all of my soon to be ex-wife (Alexis) belongings in the yard. I unload her clothing in the grass. As I'm about to step foot back into my car Alexis is pulling up in the yard with the same guy that I caught her with before. I go ballistic. My Adrenaline is pumping and I become hell on earth.

"What in the hell are you doing Terrence?" Alexis confronts me.

"I'm bringing you all your shit; you want a divorce…cool, but just know that I'm not giving you a dime"

"Terrence this is childish, you didn't have to dump all of my clothes and personal belonging out here in the yard"

"Shut the fuck up, because I am so close to snapping your neck in two pieces."

After about five minutes things between me Alexis and the guy that was still sitting in the vehicle starts to get real hectic and that's when Lisa comes strolling outside.

"You three are going to have to get the hell away from here with all that noise. I have neighbors." Lisa feuds.

"I'm sorry Lisa" Alexis explains.

"Yeh, you sorry aight! You sorry bitch" I blurt out.

"Aye man, that's not the way you talk to a lady" The man chimes in.

"Fuck you, you lucky I haven't scrubbed you up out here"

"You lucky that I'm trying not to catch a charge"

"And all of ya'll are lucky that my husband is out of town on business. Because if he was here things would not be looking good for any of ya'll"

"I don't have time for this bullshit you can have her scandalous ass dude"

"Fuck you Terrence"

"I'm sure you've been fucking ol' boys' brains out so I'll pass" I say sarcastically. "I'm out, have a nice life"

"Go to hell!" Alexis shouts.

"See you there" I tell Alexis as I step into my car, slam the car door and drive off.

23

ALEXIS

Dear Beautiful,
Whenever you need a shoulder to cry on just know that
you can always count on me. I've only known you for this
short while and the only question that I've been able to
ask myself is where you've been all of my life. You are so
much more than just a pretty face. In my eyes you are
everything a man could dream of and more. Not every-
one will be blessed with having an angel come into their
life. I hope that one day you'll give me the chance to
heal your broken heart. I don't know where we are head-
ed but I like the way we are going.
Yours Truly,
Marcus

That's the letter that was placed on the empty pillow
when I awoke in Marcus's home that morning. It had
been a week since I last spoken to Terrence, and since
that time Marcus and I were kick'n it on the regular. He

was such a gentleman. He opened the car door for me whenever we went out. He massaged my feet and gave me backrubs without me having to ask him to do it. He was interested in my dreams and he also suggested that I start my own business as a dance instructor. He was everything that I'd ever prayed for in a man. Everything was going copacetic in my life at that time even though Marcus was not bringing in anywhere close to the type of finances that I had gotten accustomed to. But that didn't matter to me. I was unemployed because Christopher used the incident that happened between me and Janice while I was at work as an excuse to terminate me. I guess that bitch Pam did not keep her promise. There was nothing that I could do about it either even though I knew that it wasn't the reason that I was fired.

I was broke, with no vehicle, no job and no plan for my future. But for the first time I was happier than I had been in a long time. I was done with Terrence and I had no plans on looking back.

Apparently Marcus had taken off earlier that morning and he didn't want to awake me. The breakfast that he'd cooked that morning was cold so I knew that he'd been away from the house for quite some time. I started me a hot shower and hopped right in. After maybe fifteen minutes I was done showering. I walked into the bedroom with the towel wrapped around me. Moments later Marcus strolled into the room.

"What's up sexy" He said munching on a strip of bacon that he'd cooked earlier that morning.

I dropped my towel to the floor revealing my

round hips, flat stomach, and firm set of tits and con-toured Marcus in closer to me. "Me on top of you" I told him as I forced him down to the bed. He laid there with his head propped up on the pillow and both of his hands behind his head. I unzipped his pants and pulled out his dick. And it was huge. The longest, thickest dick I'd ever seen. My mouth started to get juicy for it and I was ready to devour every inch of it. He flipped me upside down and I sucked his dick as he ate my pussy like it had never been eaten before. After about ten minutes of four play: my pussy was throbbing for more He flipped me over and eased inside of me doggystyle. My heart was beating fast, and the penetration was intense. It was so painful, that I started running up the bed.

"Why you running from me? Do you want me to stop?"

"No, but go easy" I told him.

"I am going easy I only have the head in"

I wanted to cry, because it was too much to get use to. *I don't know if I'm going to be able to take this I said under my breath.* But to my surprise Marcus knew just how to work his big dick so that I could feel more pleasure than pain. He coasted me over on my back and held me tight while he kissed and massaged my body, slowly stroking my vagina. All you could hear was the gushing sound of my juices overflowing as Marcus stroked, and the erotic noises I made.

"I want you to get on top" Marcus declared.

So once he lay back, I eased down on his rock hard dick and entered the head inside of me.

"I don't think I'm going to be able to do this" I told Marcus.

"It's okay, just take it easy and gradually work your way into it."

I did exactly that and even though Marcus's entire dick was not inside of me I still felt it inside of my stomach. Marcus and I had slow sensual sex that morning. When it was over I laid my head down on his chest and thought to myself Terrence WHO!!!!!!

An hour later, Marcus hopped out of the bed excitedly, and pulled me out of the bed to. I was learning him quickly and I wasn't surprised when he told me that he had a surprise for me.

"Come with me there is something that I want to show you"

"What is it?" I asked.

"It's a surprise now hurry up and get dressed"
I slid on a pair of jeans and one of Marcus's shirts and the two of us jetted to the garage. He opened the garage door and there was a Toyota Camry that he'd been repairing.

"I know that it's not what you are use to driving but it's something so that you want have to depend on anyone else"

"Marcus I can't take this car"
He handed me a set of car keys "This is what I've been out here working on all week. Take it…it's yours"

I grabbed the keys from him and jumped into his arms, like he'd just given me the keys to a jaguar. Marcus couldn't afford to give me the type of lifestyle that Terrence could but his heart was always in the right place. We both hopped into the car and took a ride around town. I was happy with my new care-free life.

Two days later Lisa and I were at Walmart shopping for a few household supplies. While we were walking around the store, I began to feel sick and very tired. I had also been sleeping a lot and was feeling rather weak. I thought that I was just overwhelmed from the recent chaos that I had been through. But when I missed my period that month and took an at home pregnancy test I found out that I was pregnant. Because of the fact that Marcus and I had always used protection and we'd recently begun having sex. It was too soon for me to be pregnant by Marcus. I was carrying Terrence's child.

Of course I was confused! Because I always wanted kids but after I was married to Terrence for a while I no longer wanted a family. For the next 2 weeks I battled with the question of should I tell Terrence that I was carrying his child or should I just have an abortion. How would I tell Marcus? The only person that I could think to call was Lisa.

"Hello there stranger" Lisa said as she answered the phone. "I haven't seen you in a while…Things must be working out pretty good between you and Marcus?"

"Hi" I said sounding a bit down. "Things won't be going good for long"

"What's wrong with you? Lisa asked worriedly.

"Lisa, I just found out that I'm pregnant by Terrence and I don't know if I should have the baby or not!"

"I would have an abortion; I wouldn't keep the baby and have to worry about dealing with Terrence...but then again I really can't say because on the other hand I would use the baby to take him for everything that he's got"

"What about Marcus?"

"What about him? Hell, it was good while it lasted."

"I don't want to hurt him."

"Do you actually think that he'll still want you when he finds out that you are carrying another man's child? I would pretend to reconcile my marriage with Terrence, have the baby and use him as my ATM machine."

"You told me that I would be a fool if I took Terrence back, and now you're telling me to take him back."

"That was before a baby came into play"

"You think I ought to use this baby to get to Terrence's money"

"Hell yeh, women do it all the time. Give his ass what he deserves, but girl I'll call you back later I'm getting dressed for work"

I was confused and didn't know whether or not Lisa wanted me to be happy? She was the one that told me to get involved with Marcus but as I thought more and more about Lisa's advice I was convinced that she was right. *Marcus probably wouldn't want to have anything to do with me after I tell him that I'm carrying Terrance's child anyway.* I thought to myself.

So by now I guess you've figured out that I moved back into the house with Terrence. I know…I know, it was a dumb move, but at that time it seemed like the best thing to do. Terrance had vowed that family was going to be his number one priority, and that he was going to do right by me and our child.

I couldn't bring myself to tell Marcus that I was back with Terrence because I didn't want to hurt him. Marcus called me for nearly two weeks and I refused to answer, and I didn't expect that he would just pop up at Lisa's house without speaking with me first. Terrence and I were invited to a party at Lisa's house and I was in the kitchen whipping up my famous nacho dip that everyone loves when I heard Terrence yelling.

"What is going on" I asked as I walked in the foyer. I was completely shocked when I saw Marcus standing there.

"What in the hell is this man doing coming over here Alexis?" Terrence asked me.

"He's just a friend" I answered hesitantly.
The look on Marcus's face is a look that I will never forget. He looked as though he'd just lost his best friend.

"Oh, I'm just a friend now?" Marcus asked me.

"Terrence and I are back together"

"You weren't woman enough to tell me?" Marcus asked angrily. Where was he when you were catching the bus and crying all night with a broken heart?"

"Look you better get the hell on or I have something that will make you leave" Terrence snapped at Marcus.

"So that's it huh? What about the plans for the dance studio."

"You made plans to be with him?" Terrence asked me irately.

I just stood there not uttering one word because I was in fear of what Terrence might do if I answered the question truthfully. I'd already told him the lie that Marcus and I had never been intimate.

"Answer me," Terrence demanded.

I still did not say one word and that's when Terrance attempted to strike me. Marcus then swung at Terrence in my defense, knocking him to the floor. They got into a big tussle and I got in the middle of it to try and break up the fight. Because of the strength of the two men I was knocked to the floor. I was crying in pain, before Marcus and Terrance realized that I was on the floor in a cradle position. Marcus ran to my aid and Terrence didn't even bother. Instead he ran out of the house in a rage.

"Marcus I'll be okay. Just leave he's going to his car to get his gun"

"I'm not worried about that" Marcus responded trying to pick me up off the floor.

"Terrence baby what are you doing?" I said noticing that he was barging back in the house with his gun.

"Is that supposed to scare me?" Marcus asked.

"Terrence baby he's about to go don't do anything crazy"

"Baby, don't let him fool you. This scary ass nigga won't last one day in prison. He ain't gon' do shit"

"Terrence baby please think about the future. Think about the baby"

"The baby" Marcus mutters.

"Yeh I found out that I'm six weeks pregnant."

"Alexis shut the hell up you don't have to explain nothing to that low life."

"And you want to be with someone that speaks to you that way?" Marcus asked. "I feel sorry for that poor kid."

Marcus tried to persuade me to leave Terrence; he tried even harder because I was pregnant. I refuse to listen. A couple of days later I returned the car to Marcus.

In no time, my life was back to the way that it once was. Meaning Terrence was still the same old Terrence. Staying out all night, and claiming that he was working. Only this time things were ten times worst because I was pregnant and I was more fragile than normal. Anything that he said to me would hurt my feelings, and this was not good for the baby. We weren't having sex because my hormones were all out of wack and I was never in the mood to be intimate with him.

One night that I was getting ready for bed he tried to have sex with me but I wasn't in the mood and his remark was "It's cool; because what you won't do another woman will love to do."

"Don't think that you are the only one that can fuck around" I said boldly.

"Don't get fucked up in here Alexis"

"Whatever, Terrence" I climbed into the bed.

"What are you trying to say?"

"Exactly what I said"

"Let me find out that the baby that you're carrying is that broke motherfuckers' baby it's going to be hell to pay."

Six months later at a little over seven months pregnant Terrence and I still hadn't touched each other, but I knew that he was getting sex from someone.

24

LISA

For the life of me, I can't understand what is so special about Alexis. I envy her and I'm thrilled to know that Terrence is sticking it to her ass. And you want to know what else? I've been a big part of their marital problems.

See me and Terrence go back long before he met Alexis. Just like most men, he was instantly attracted to her, but I was in love with him and I wasn't about to let her take him away from me. That's why I never stopped screwing him.

I've been fucking my supposedly best friend's husband the entire time she's been married to him, which is kind of crazy because if my husband was to ever find out he'll have both of us killed.

I'm the one who orchestrated the whole plot, Alexis getting her ass kicked in my salon, and the infidelity between Janice and Terrence. I told her the name of the gym that Terrence was a member of. She went there every day until she finally spotted him there. I only wanted her to destroy his marriage, but she had plans of her own. When it all went down, she ended up pregnant by the man that I was in love with it. She was never supposed to sleep with him, she was only supposed to stalk him and make Alexis think that they were having an affair.

King Pen, my husband, can't fuck worth of two cents. I only married him for his money. The sex is dreadful, and most of the time he gets his rocks off from oral sex. Because having sex with him is like watching paint dry (boring as hell). On the days that I do decide to give 'em some of my good stuff he always says or does something that turns me off. Like take this for an example, he asked me to purr for him one time during a sexual encounter. My facial expression showed him that I wasn't up for any bullshit like that. What I really wanted to say to him was *"Why don't you give me something to purr about"* Not that I'm into purring anyhow. But I hate when a man thinks that he's doing something in the bedroom and isn't doing a damn thing.

Now Terrence he's another story in itself. He knows how to lay down the pipe. I've never had anyone better. No matter if it's orally or physically he gets the job done. That's why I want to be with him. Janice was supposed to be doing my dirty work but she called me the other day stating that she was done with fucking with Terrence because he was trying to gain sole custody of their son. She also told me that if I wanted Terrence's marriage destroyed I would have to take matters into my

156

own hands. And that's what I'm going to do. Sometimes in order to win the game you have to play the cards the right way, which means that I have to play dirty.

Being that Alexis trusts me she's told me all about Marcus and how he put it down between the sheets. She's also told me that she wasn't honest with Terrence when he asked if she'd been involved with Marcus sexually. I'm going to tell Terrence everything and I'm going to add a little damage to it. I know that Alexis is not pregnant by Marcus but I'm going to tell Terrence the complete opposite. Alexis and Marcus hasn't been intimate but a few times and they always used protection according to her but because I want Terrence all to myself I'm going to have to lie my way to his heart.

My doorbell rang just as I was dialing Terrence's number to see what time he would be stopping by, since King Pen was out of town on business. I raced to the door with the speed of a NASCAR race convention. Terrence was the only person, I thought that it could be, because I'd already talked to Alexis earlier that day and she told me that she would be spending the day with her parents. King pen's flight was scheduled to leave hours earlier. And it was too early in the day for Moesha to be out. A sensual feeling took over my body as I eagerly opened the door. But it was surely not the person that I wanted it to be and my mood quickly went sour.

"Hey sweetie" King Pen's mother said as she walked past me once she stepped into the house with her luggage.

"Hello Mrs. Taylor, how are you" I asked as I gave her a fake smile.

"It looks like you are surprised to see me"

"I'm just shocked I didn't know that you were in town"

"My son didn't tell you that I was coming?"

"No he hasn't told me anything about it"

"That crazy son of mines! She joked. I'm so happy that I get to spend some time with my favorite daughter in law"

"I'm so happy to spend time with you to" I continued, lying through my teeth.

I grabbed her luggage and showed her to the guest room. Once I had her situated I phoned Terrence and told him that we would have to catch up later. Our secret spot was in my pool house. And once my mother in law was sound asleep I was going to sneak outside and meet Terrence at our usual location.

The sounds of Terrence's voice richoshades off of the wall as we are being spontaneous in the pool house in the back of the home that I share with my husband.

"That's it"

"Suck it slow"

"Ooooohhhhhh"

"Damn you make me feel so good"

"Aawwhhhhh"

"Speed it up a little"

"Now grab my balls"

"I'm about to cum"

I swallow every drop like I'm drinking water from a fountain. I love making love to Terrence's dick with my mouth. I love the noises that he makes and the expression on his face when I'm serving him up. I love the feeling I get when I'm sucking him so good that his toes curls.

"You're the best" He says once it's over.

"So are you" I tell him.

I walk into the bathroom and brush and goggle my teeth. Terrence comes in and grabs me from behind.

"When am I going to see you again?"

"That depends on how long my husband is going to be out of town this time"

"Are you going to call me and let me know?"

"Of course, but I think that we should cut back until my mother in law leaves"

"Definitely because I was more nervous than a man on trial for murdering someone of the law when you snuck me up in here" We both laugh.

Terrence kisses me on my neck and I break away from him.

"What's wrong?" He asks.

"There is something that I need to tell you"

"What's on your mind?"

"The baby that Alexis is carrying may not be yours"

"What? He starts breathing hard as he forms his hand into a fist.

"I've been trying to figure out a way to tell you that there is a possibility that Marcus could be the father."

159

"Did she tell you that?"

"Yeh she told me that they had unprotected sex in your house"

Terrence punches the mirror in the bathroom. Luckily it didn't shatter.

"I'm going to kill her"

"Terrence calm down" I assert.

"Calm down…this is not something that I can calm down about; she looked me dead in my eyes and lied to me"

"Terrence, I'm sorry she lied to you, but think about it, me and you we can just run away together"

He starts to cry, as he destroys everything in sight. His eyes are blood shot red and I realize that maybe it wasn't a good idea to tell him those lies. He's probably going to hurt Alexis really bad.

"You know I saw my dad go through this as a child and I never thought it would be me" He breaks down to his knees and cries loudly. I kneel down beside him and start caressing his head. I grab him and hug him tightly. "Everything is going to be okay" I assure him.

Once, he regained his composure he absconded out of the house.

25

ALEXIS

"Terrence please, let me go you're hurting me" I begged as Terrence dragged me down the hallway in our home. I was seven months pregnant and getting my ass whipped by my husband for a reason that was unbeknownst to me. There was no way that I could break loose. I thought for sure that he was going to kill me. He'd already slapped me down to the floor as soon as he stepped foot into the living room. "Lying ass bitch" he kept repeating. I had no clue where all the anguish was coming from; neither did I know what I'd done so terribly wrong.

"Terrence, please stop. I'm carrying your child" I begged.

Terrence picked me up by neck and I gagged for air. He then threw me into the wall, and stood directly in front of me. "So you fucked ol' boy and lied to me about it?"

"What are you talking about?" I acted dumb-founded

"You know what the hell I'm talking about"

"I've already told you, I haven't been with anyone but you since we've been married."

"Quit lyyyiinnnnnng to me" He yelled.
Tears rolled down his cheeks, and I feared for my life. I was torn between whether I should confess or tell a lie, because I didn't know how much information Terrence knew or where he even got his information from. While I was hemmed up on the wall, my head was in a million different places and I had no choice but to come clean about everything.

"Look it happened once okay but we used protec-tion" I was then slapped down to the floor. My nose was bleeding as he punched me over and over again. I became tired of trying to get away so I took a deep breath and prepared myself for blow after blow. That's exactly what he gave me until he'd tired himself out and left the house.

After the beating my puffy eyes, were bruised and black-ened. My nose felt like it had broken in six different places, and my stomach was in excruciating pain. I checked for my teeth because I was sure that he'd broken my jaw but they were all in place. I crawled into the bath-room and started a bubble bath. Surprisingly I was able to help myself into the tub.

Once I was done bathing my muscles were relaxed a little but still remained sore. My stomach was throbbing more than anything else. It was the worst pain I'd ever experienced. But I toughed it out because I had to get out of the house and I didn't want to call anyone for help because I knew that they'd want to call the police.

I gathered all of my things, along with my unborn child belongings and packed them tightly in my car. I refused to give him back the Bentley, I figured he didn't need all those vehicles; He had the Corvette, and the Rover. With that being said I placed my house key and wedding ring on the night stand drawer in our bedroom. Then I collected the nine millimeter for protection in case Terrence and I were to cross paths, checked it to make sure that it was on safety and stuck it in my Gucci tote bag. When I left the house that day I knew deep down in my soul that it was going to be the end of that chapter in my life.

My baby was due in less than two months and at the time I didn't have a pot to piss in or a window to throw it out as my mama would say. I needed a plan, and I needed one quickly.

In the back of my mind I was wondering could Lisa have been the one that told Terrence about Marcus and me. But the more I thought about it I told myself that Lisa would never betray me like that.

The only person that I could go to was Jody. And the reason why was because he was the only friend that I had, whom Terrence had no idea where he lived. So that's where I headed the day I decided to walk away from it all.

26

TERRENCE

My behavior was out of control. But I completely
blanked out. Although I was crushed by what Lisa confessed to me, it's not an excuse for what I've done to
Alexis. Lisa's news kept playing back in my head and I
couldn't control my behavior. Those memories from
when I was a young boy were the only thing in my mind.
All I could think about was my mother, and what she'd
done to my father. I remembered how I felt when I witnessed her sneaking different guys out of my dad's
house. Animosity transformed me into a monster as I pictured her fucking another man in my bed. Then I
wondered was he the only person that she'd been with
during our marriage. I became angrier as I thought about
how she'd been so conniving, but yet look so innocent,
and tell me that she'd never had sex with him.

While driving home I told myself that I was going to calm down and not do anything that I would regret afterwards. But once I walked through the front door of our house and I saw her lying on the sofa asleep in the family room. The only thing that I could picture was how another man had fucked her, and unprotected at that, possibly in that very room. Hell I didn't know. All I know is that she was in my house when she fucked him. I gritted my teeth and tried to ignore the flashbacks that were easing up in my mind. I battled with my demons four about twenty minutes before I lost the war. I spased out and the next thing I knew I was pulling Alexis off the sofa by her feet. I dragged her down the hall and up the stairs as she begged for me to stop. I repeatedly asked her "Why did you lie to me?" She constantly acted bamboozled. I became more and more furious every time that she lied. I grabbed her by the neck and pounded her up against the wall in our bedroom. Finally she whimpered. "Look it happened once okay but we used protection" Tears of pain trickled down my face as I threw her down onto the floor. The smart as comment she made months ago replayed in my head like a track that's on repeat. *"Don't think that you are the only one that can fuck around"* I looked at her round belly, and, couldn't come to terms with the fact that it could be someone else's baby that she's carrying. I beat her like she wasn't the woman I married. She begged me to stop, but I couldn't.

When I came back to, the punches stopped and I couldn't believe what I'd done. I wanted to take it all back. But it wasn't like I could just press rewind and start

166

all over again. She was bloody and bruised. She wasn't crying any more as she lay there silently. I tried to help her but I couldn't get her to move. She lay there as if she was paralyzed. I apologized to her, and I didn't know what else to do besides leave.

I was sure that she would be calling the police so that's why I'm hanging out over at Lisa's. She'll probably call Lisa but she want stop by because she thinks that I will come by here to find her. I'm pretty sure that she's going to be leaving me now. So I've prepared myself.

After this marriage is over I'm going to be through with relationships, so all of this bullshit that Lisa is blabbing about in my ear at the moment is not making any since to me. Ever since I gave her the whole rundown of how I reacted to what she'd told me, she's been convinced that Alexis and I were done and that she and I should run off and be together. Fuck no! What do I look like, a fool? I've fucked her for the last past 6 years in her pool house while her husband is out on business. What in the hell makes her think that I want to be in a relationship with her. I don't trust her any further than I can throw her. She's just another woman that I use for sex. For me there aren't any feelings involved. The only feelings she can ever expect to get from me is the feeling she gives me when she's damn near sucking the skin off of my manhood. That's it! If she knows what's best she wouldn't walk away from her marriage. She's married to a big time drug dealer, who has the street power, to have her found some where stinking if she tries to leave him.

She probably knows too much and to keep her from air-
ing out his dirty laundry he'll probably have someone to
get rid of her.

Listen to me talk about he'll have someone to kill
Lisa, because if he were to ever find out that I've been
fucking his wife in his pool house, my ass will be found
dead right along with her. Several occasions I've tried to
walk away from my affair with Lisa but the relishing
feeling of her mouth always calls me back. The only way
that I can get away from everything is by moving away
and that's exactly what I plan on doing.

If the baby that Alexis is carrying turns out to be
my kid, I'll just put the money in her account, and I'll do
the same thing for Janice. I need a fresh start.

27

ALEXIS

"Jody…. Jody open the door" I yelled as I knocked on the door of Jody's condo. It was late and I was sure that he was asleep. But I needed him. I fled over to his spot as soon as I left my home. After maybe about five minutes of constant knocking on the door Jody finally answered.

"Who is it?"

"Alexis"

Jody snatched open the door and stood between the crack of it "Girl…why you knocking on my door like you the damn police?"

"I need your help. I need to crash here tonight" I let myself into his apartment.

Jody and I both went into the living room. He turned on a lamp as we entered, which I hated because he had a clearer look at the bruises on my face.

"What happened to your face?" Jody pointed out.

"Terrence came home tonight questioning me about Marcus and ended up kicking my ass"

"Did you call the police?"

"Nah and I don't want to either"

"That's got to be the dumbest shit I've ever heard." Jody said as he gave me a serious look.

I rolled my eyes at him.

"Do you realize how foolish you sound right now?"

"I don't want Terrence to get arrested, so I'm not going to get the police involved but I am going to leave him for sure this time" I tried to explain.

"Fuck that, you got arrested behind his bullshit"

"That wasn't his fought; he didn't put a gun to my head and make me continuously ram my car into the back of his."

"There you go again always trying to make up excuses for him. Somebody needs to kick his ass. Got you running over here in the middle of the night beating on my goddamn door, while I'm trying to spend some quality time with my man"

"Oooh… that is too much information."

"And you put up with too much bullshit, you need to get a backbone honey. Hell, look at your face. I want to roll out and kick his ass myself."

I walked over to the sofa and sat down. I hung my head low, covered my face with both hands and cried loudly. Jody walked over and sat down beside me. He rubbed my back gently in an effort to comfort me.

"Don't cry. You're going to be okay but you have to erase that asshole out of your life for good. He doesn't mean you any good."

"I know that, but what am I supposed to do? I don't have a job, any savings, a place to stay. I don't have anything and my baby is due in two months.

"I hate to say that I told you so. I warned you that if you and Terrence divorced that he was going to leave you with nothing. My door is always open and I'll do whatever I can do for you and your baby to make sure that you never think twice about going back to Terrence.

"Thanks Jody I don't know what I would do if I didn't have a friend like you"

"Everything is going to work itself out. As soon as you drop that load you will be able to start working again and get back on your feet. But this time do it on your own, without a man."

I smiled at Jody and he leaned over and gave me a sympathetic kiss on my cheek before he said "goodnight"

I yawned. "Good-night"

"Alright love we'll definitely finish this conversation later. Help yourself to whateva' you want, you know where the kitchen is."

Jody walked away but returned seconds later with a blanket for me to keep warm with. "You want the light off?"

"Yeh" I told him.

"See you in the a.m." Jody said as switched off the lamp and exited.

"Thanks again Jody"

Later, I was awoken out of a deep sleep. Apparently Jody was getting his freak on. I wiggled around on the sofa for a little bit, and I did my best to ignore the sounds that were coming from Jody's bedroom. I glanced at my watch and it was 5:00 in the morning.

"Yeah suck daddy's dick good" I heard a guy saying before I heard a long exotic scream from pleasure. Jody had given the man some lip service. And the thought of it made my stomach turn inside out, because I knew that he was fucking some woman's husband. Those are the only type of guys that he messed around with. I loved Jody like family and his sexual preference was his business not mines, but I didn't agree with him having sex with married men. Because I would have lost my mind if I were to ever find out that Terrence was sleeping around with a man.

Moments later I heard Jody's bedroom door open. He was having a conversation with the man as they walked down the hall. I pretended to be asleep, but I didn't have my eyes completely closed because I wanted to get a glimpse of the man. He was a dark skinned guy. With the appearance of a thug he was dressed in all black. His dread locks were pulled back into a ponytail. To society he would never have come off as a guy that was on the down low. He and Jody both walked outside.

I eased up a little almost into a seating position and peeped out of the window that was above the sofa where I was sleeping so that I could get a better view of the man. He resembled King Pen and once I saw Lisa's car pull up and he got inside of it. I knew that it was him.

I was shocked. The thought of my best friend's husband turning out to be a queer was a bit much. I couldn't faither the anguish and humility she would feel once she found out about her husband and Jody. He was supposed to be out of town on business. Instead his gri-my ass had someone drop him off at Jody's place, so that he could keep his shit on the down low. Immediately af-ter Jody walked through the front door I called him into the living room.

"Girl what are you still doing up?"

"Well it was kinda' hard to stay asleep with all of the moaning and groaning I heard"

"My baacckkk" Jody laughed.

"Jody I have to ask you a serious question"

"I'm listening"

"Do you know that the man that just left is Lisa's husband?"

"Oh no, that can't be true because he's not mar-ried"

"Yes he is, his name is King Pen"

Jody's expression changes. "For once I thought that I'd finally met someone that wasn't married."

"I hate to be the barrel of bad news but he's mar-ried to Lisa"

"Or you sure?"

"Of course! I couldn't get a good look at him, but I'm pretty sure that he is Lisa's husband. What kind of car did he leave in?"

"I believe that it was a Jaguar"

"That was Lisa's car. How long have the two of you been messing around?"

"About six months"

"Dang I can't believe this" I sighed. "You know I have to Tell Lisa right?"

"That's fine, tell her. She's your friend not mines. It's not like I knew that he was her man."

"Well did the two of you use protection?"

"Almost never"

That's when everything that I had eaten that day came back out of me. Luckily there was a trash can close by.

"You okay?" Jody asked.

"I'm fine I'm just overwhelmed with everything that's all" I was bent over head first into the trash can.

"I'm going back to bed" Jody informed me.

He walked out of the living room and just like that our conversation was over.

28

LISA

It was twenty minutes to seven o'clock am and I was sitting at the foot of the bed, in the pool house when Terrence told me that it was time that we ended our six year affair. That instant I became sad and I couldn't understand why. I'd been drilling in his head that we needed to run away together ever since he came back after his dispute with Alexis. I wanted him to be mines, I wanted us to have kids and live happily ever after. He was totally against it. He told me that he didn't look at me that way. My heart felt like it broke in one million different pieces, and the only way that it could be puzzled back together was if he were to tell me that he didn't mean any of it.

Our wonderful sex life had come to end. What was I supposed to do from then on? Besides my husband, Terrence was the only person that I was being intimate with. Surely I couldn't live the rest of my life faking orgasms. So I put up a pretty strong argument with Terrence.

"What's gotten into you? Why do you want to walk away from me after all of these years?"

"Things are just getting out of control."

"Terrence Please don't cut me out of your life" I begged him.

"Look…I'm seriously thinking about moving away. I'm thinking about moving back home for a little while. I need some space"

"I love you. Don't you love me?"

"Lisa I'm not going to lie I enjoy our sex life but for me it's nothing more than that. You're feelings only proves that things have gotten out of hand"

"Terrence we go back so many years, you must feel something:"

"Lisa it's over" He stood up from the bed and walked over to the pool house door and cracked it open.

"I thought that you said that you were going to lay low at my place for a little while?"

He turns around and walks into the bathroom. I follow closely behind him crying as I demand that we make love one last time. He does his best to resist the sloppy wet kisses that I plant on his neck. I pull up his T-shirt and lick his chest as I circle my tongue around his nipple. He starts moaning as he forces my head down to his manhood. I unbuckle his jeans and perform oral sex like I'm in a dick sucking contest and the grand prize is ten million dollars. I have the power over him in this very

176

moment. He squirms and jerks as I suck fast, then slow making damn sure that I'm serving him up a platter of his best lip service.

"I'm going to miss this" He tells me.
That's exactly what I want to hear. Maybe he'll change his mind.

"Let me hit that pussy for the last time" he lustfully dictates as he pulls me up from off of my knees. He pushes down the toilet seat and sits down. His pants are pulled down to his feet. He slides my thong over to one side and coaches me onto his lap. I rotate my hips around as he cuffs my breast in his hand. "Ahh" He moans. "Ride it slower" He dictates.

We are both sweating, as we are in awe of our sex. I mean, our sexual chemistry is like picking an apple from an orange tree...like Alaska with 80 degree weather in December...like...okay, never mind. You should get my drift. Our sex is unbelievable. It's amazing how our bodies just hymn together at the same tone, rhythm and vibe. When his dick is inside of me, suddenly I can speak every language that there is. We'll at least that's how it seems...because right now I'm speaking in tongue, and that's a new one, even for me.

I hear footsteps walking around in the living room of the pool house and my heart jumps out of my chest. Terrence and I are both nude as the door swings opens.

"Look I can explain" I say.
I scramble to my feet and try to collect my clothing. Terrence pulls up his pants.

29

ALEXIS

I banged on the front door to Lisa's house and she didn't answer. I knew that she was there because her car was in the driveway. So, I figured that she was out back in the pool house, because I noticed that the lights were on. Upon my arrival to the pool house, the door was slightly cracked, so I let myself in. "Where you at Lisa" I yelled. That's when I heard her moaning. I was just about to walk out when I heard a groan coming from a guy. The reason I stood there in disarray was because I'd heard that groan before. I was familiar with it. I walked closer to where the noise was coming from and opened the door.

My heart along with my mind wasn't prepared for what I'd just witnessed. I dropped my Gucci tote to the floor. It seemed like the room was spinning as I tried to rationalize with the situation.

"Look I can explain" Lisa stated as she attempted to get dress.

"Alexis, this isn't what it looks Like" Terrence concluded. Without saying anything I kneeled down and grabbed the nine millimeter, took the safety off of it, wiped the tears from my eyes, pointed the gun towards the ceiling and pulled the trigger. Terrence and Lisa both ducked. I locked the bathroom door and dared them both to budge.

"I don't want to hear anything that the two of you have to say, as a matter of fact take your clothes back off Lisa. You didn't have a problem being naked before I walked in here, so take them off" I shouted angrily before I looked over at Terrence with a revengeful stare.

"Take yours off to" I told Terrence. "So how long has this been going on Terrence" And you better not lie because I'm going to blow your fucking head off"

They were both standing there naked, trembling in fear of their life. I could sense that they were uncomfortable standing there in the nude. Lisa suddenly became bold and grabbed her under garments and attempted to put them back on. "This is just plain out crazy" She stated.

"Bitch did I tell you to move. You didn't seem to have a problem being naked before I entered the room so keep that same attitude because I'm gon' beat your scandalous ass just like that, as soon as I kill Terrence." I struck Lisa across the face with the gun. Terrence was sitting there looking as if he wanted to jump into her defense. This only pissed me off more, so I questioned him.

"Oh so you hate the fact that I pistle whipped your little bitch?" I yelled before I struck him across the head with gun.

"Uhh my head hurts Alexis" Lisa cried out, as she pulled her bloody hand down from her face and glanced at it.

"There couldn't be a person in this world that could care less about you being in pain. Look at how you've hurt me."

"Your ass is crazy as hell" Terrence stated.

"Trust me, you haven't seen crazy yet." I said tapping the gun upside my head. Then I looked over at Lisa and began combing the gun down her hair. "Let me take a wild guess you're the one that told Terrence about Marcus and I?"

She nodded her head yes.

"And you also told him, that the baby that I'm carrying is not his. Even though you know that it is? Because I told you that Marcus and I always used protection"

Terrence looked shocked. "You lied to me?"

She didn't answer the question.

"Answer the question bitch" I shouted. "I want you to tell the truth. Tell Terrence that you lied to him"

"I lied about everything Terrence, I made it all" she muttered.

"You see Terrence you came home and beat the hell out of me because this bitch filled your head up with lies, and now I'm standing here all banged up. So answer this question Terrence, how long has this bitch been feeding you lies about me?"

He turned to Lisa with a disgusted expression on his face and answered. "For our entire marriage"

"So you've been fucking my man all this time? Bitch open your mouth" I told Lisa as I forced the gun in her mouth. "Yeh suck on that like you've been sucking on my man for all these years"

Tears rolled down the side of Lisa's cheeks because she was in fear that I was going to kill her.

"That doesn't feel so good does it? Well you see the way I'm feeling right now it's…it's not good" I stuttered. "I feel betrayed, my best friend and my husband. How could you do this to me?" I was crying heavily. "You know how much I love Terrence!" I took the gun out of Lisa's mouth and let off another shot into the bathroom ceiling.

I then turned to Terrence and pistil whipped him until he tried to gain control of the gun. I let off another shot missing him intentionally. I just wanted him to be aware of the fact that I was in control of the ship. I was the captain and he was to follow my orders. But then I was hit with a dose of reality. "Oh my God" I said aloud. I became dizzier. "If King Pen has been fucking Jody, and Lisa's been fucking King Pen. You have been fucking her, and I have been fucking you. That means that we all could be in some serious trouble." I stated.

Terrence's face was turned upside down as his expression looked like he wanted to just vomit all over the place. "King Pen has been fucking Jody?"

"Yes, that's what I was coming over here to tell Lisa"

A horrible pain started to form in my stomach all over again. Immediately I fainted.

"I think that I'm having labor pains" I cried out painfully once I regained consciousness.

Terrence was kneeled down beside me. "Alexis you need to let me take you to the hospital"

"I'm okay"

"No, you need to let me take you to the hospital"

"Why do you continuously hurt me?"

"Never mind all of that right now" Terrence lifted me from the floor.

While I was on the floor I was holding my stomach and screaming. "I think I'm having contractions"

"It's too soon for all of that. It's probably just a short pain from the fall when you passed out."

"The baby is not going to make it" I cried.

"Don't think like that just stay calm. The Baby is going to be okay."

Terrence carried me in his arms outside to his car and drove me to the hospital.

30

LISA

After I heard the pool house door close, I knew that it was the end of my romance with Terrence. I cleaned my face and grabbed the Aleve bottle from the medicine cabinet. I quickly chased down two caplets with tap water from the bathroom sink. My head was spinning, and I became dizzy, so I took a seat on the bathroom floor. It was early in the morning so I was shocked that the phone was ringing.

"Hello" I said.

"Why did you tell me all of those lies?"

"I don't know, I guess I was just that desperate to have you. I'm sorry" I confessed to Terrence.

"Sorry is not going to cut it. From this day forward I may as well be dead to you"

"Terrence I did it for you, she doesn't deserve you. She'll never love you the way I do, please don't do this to me."

"Woman you have lost your mind" He pauses before he clears his throat because his voice is now hoarse. He continues. "There is nothing that you can say to me to convince me to continue fucking around with you. If you lied about something this serious I would hate to find out what else you've lied about"

"Terrence I'm in love with you"

Janice is calling me on the other end. And I need to talk to her especially since I've been calling her for a few weeks and I haven't been able to reach her.

"Will you hold on for a sec" I ask Terrence.

"Goodbye Lisa" He hangs up.

I click over to Janice.

"Hey girl, where have you been?"

"I've been around"

"I've been calling you why haven't you been returning my calls?"

"I told you I was done with your scandals against Terrence. Besides I have a lot on my mind right now"

"Like what?"

"Like HIV"

There was silence on the phone.

"Did you hear me? I said I have HIV"

"Welcome to my world" I told her.

"Excuse you?"

"Yeh, you heard me. Welcome to my world."

"So you already knew that you were sick with this disease?"

"How could I not know? I'm married to a man that lives his life on the down low, and dares me to leave him"

"I can't believe you dragged me into your misery"

"Well you know what they say, misery loves company"

"Since you think that what you've done to me is okay. How about I call King Pen and tell him how you've been fucking Terrence in your pool house for years."

"Tell him because by the time you contact him I'll be on a plane to another country"

"You are one crazy ass bitch. You're just going to travel the world destroying other people's lives. I hate you. My cousin is in a nut house because she tried to kill herself after she found out that she was positive. And you don't even care."

"King Pen didn't care when he gave it to me" I informed her.

CLICK. I hang up.

I have known that King Pen fucks other men for about two years now ever since I walked in on him receiving head from a cross-dresser in a hotel room, one time that I called myself trying to surprise him when he was away on one of his business trips. He was surprised alright, and so was I. He told me that he would have my brains blown out if I told anyone. And I never told a soul. He also dared me to divorce him, because he thought that

185

I was going to leave and take everything with me, being that everything he owned is in my name.

I have been living with HIV for about four years. And of course I contracted it from my husband. I know that I should have told Terrence years ago, but I look at this way, no one told me, so why not spread the love.

It's time for me to move on with my life. Meaning I guess it's going to be a lot of motherfuckers walking around with that AIDS package.

The very next day, I left everything... my car, my home, clothes, jewelry, and my entire life in Atlanta GA. I cleared out the bank account, although it wasn't my money. How would King Pen prove that it was his? The account was listed in my name and my name only.

Now I travel all around the world, still spreading the love. I once would have loved to spend King Pen's money with Terrence by my side, but spending it without him feels even better.

31

ALEXIS

When we arrived to the hospital it was nothing that they could do to stop my labor. After being in labor for only one hour I gave birth to a two pound baby girl. She was the same complexion as me, with gray eyes and sandy red hair. She was breath-taking.

Terrence and I had decided months earlier that if I birthed a girl we would name her Angel Mariah Johnson. After she'd been in the hospital for two months I was finally able to take her home.

Being that I didn't have a home of my own, I had no choice but to move in with my parents. I loved being a mother; I just hated the fact that I didn't have any help. Terrence was always out and about, while my life now revolved around our child. He stopped by every once and a while to see her. I never had any time to myself, unless my mother volunteered to watch her for a few hours. On those days I didn't get the chance to do anything. Because I was too tired, and would just lounge around the house.

My annual check-ups were always petrifying because I was always anticipating that I'd be told that I was HIV positive. Janice informed Terrence that she was positive and shockingly he told me about it. After every visit I always left relieved because my blood test was normal.

Terrence was a doctor and wouldn't get tested. How crazy was that? He would always say that he would rather not know. He continued to fuck around with different women, possibly infecting them, but he didn't care. He was just heartless like that. And because of that I didn't want him around my daughter.

Two years had passed and my blood test was still negative. Marcus and I were back together and we were living in a house that Marcus had built from the ground up. It was a gorgeous four bedroom home. Business was going rather well for Marcus and he was able to afford a decent lifestyle for his son, Angel, and I. Angel was walking, talking, and being a normal toddler, and her dad was still acting like an asshole. "I don't want my baby around your bitch ass boyfriend" He always said. We'd been going through an elongated custody battle for about a year in a half…and boy was I ready for it to be over with.

Divorcing Terrence did not stand alone-because this decision came with some disastrous consequences. There were several occasions where Marcus and Terrance would have disputes. This situation was really taking a toll on Angel. Really and truly I wish that I had a choice of rather or not Terrence had the right to see her. Each time we were in each other's site there would always be a quarrel. I would get a feeling of disgust at the sight of his presence but Angel on the other hand; acted as if he was a superstar. Angel had formed multiple attachments and bonds with both of us. She wanted to spend just as much time with Terrence as she spent with me. He'd been saying that he was going to move back to his hometown ever since Angel was born but the asshole never moved. Instead he hired expensive Lawyers to make sure that I didn't walk away with anything and after a tiresome and bothersome battle in court I was awarded both of the cars, that Terrence had taken back from me, the house, which I declined, and eighty thousand dollars, a year in alimony and child support and also half of Terrence's pension. This ruling infuriated him. He became a man with no self- control.

"This was all in your plan; you're nothing but a gold digging bitch. How could you do this to me? If it weren't for me your parents would still be struggling to pay for your education" Terrence shouted to me after our final court date.

"All this is your fault" I told him. "If it weren't for you, and my parents trying to control every move I made in my life I wouldn't be in the situation that I'm in right now because I would have moved to New York and I never would have met your trifling ass."

There was no compromising with Terrence and I had begun to hate the day I ever met him.

It was a Sunday and it was Terrence's week to have Angel and my plan was to take her to his house when church was over. Unfortunately Terrence was being difficult. I pulled my phone out of my purse to check it for messages, when we were leaving the church grounds and I had a text from Terrence. *Alexis I told you that I was coming to pick Angel up this morning so you need to answer the damn phone.*

Just as I was calling him back his number appeared on my caller I.D.

"Terrence I told you that I would bring Angel to you" I hollered in the phone. "I'm on my way over there." I yelled. I hung up the phone in his face.

Angel was in the back seat minding her own business as she dug into the McDonald's bag. I flushed the pedal to floor, fleeing to Terrence's house.

Once I pulled up he was standing on the porch. He walked down the steps and towards my car. I assumed that he was coming to help get Angels bags out of the car. So I stepped out and walked around to get Angel out of the car seat. Once I'd kneeled down to unstrap the carseat. He snatched me away from the car and tossed me down to the ground. He brutally kicked me in the stomach.

"Stop hurting mommy daddy." Angel cried.

"You think that you something now, hanging up in my face stupid bitch"

"Terrence, why are you doing this in front of Angel? Your scaring her, I said curled up in a fetal position.

"Yeh, you deserve this, riding around in my god-damn car." He roared as he continued to stump me.

My back was turned away from my car so I couldn't see that Angel had gotten out of the car to try and help me.

"Stop hitting my mommy" She cried as she pounded her dad in his back.

He used his forearm and trampled Angel down to the ground. She fell backwards and her head slammed into the hard pavement.

"Mommyyyyyyyy" She cried.

My mind went blank and before I knew it I kicked Terrence as hard as I could in his balls. He bent down in pain and grabbed himself with both of his hands before he fell onto the concrete. I then grabbed Angel and sprinted to my car. I felt deep down in my soul that Terrence was going to kill me if I didn't leave. I did not want to pull out the gun because Angel was with me, and she had already heard and seen enough. Before I could pull off Terrence was pulling on the handle of the car door.

"Open the fucking door bitch"

"Daddy please stop" Angel screamed.

"Open the damn door Alexis before I shatter this window" Terrence demanded.

"Terrence you're scaring Angel please calm down"

"You started this Alexis and now I'm going to finish it" He yelled, now kicking the door.

"Terrence I have the gun in here and I don't want to have to use it. Please I just want to get Angel home safely"

"Oh Angel is ok 'but your life is going to end today" Terrence shouted.

I began to panic. I was not ready to die yet. I was still young I was only twenty nine years old.

By the grace of God Terrence snapped into terms with what he was about to do and said "You know what you're not worth everything that I have worked hard for" He stormed away and Angel and I drove off because there was no way that I was going to leave my child with him.

As you know along with happiness there comes pain. In my case it was Chasity. How in the hell do men pick their women? I will never understand how a man as generous, respectful, and charming as Marcus could have a child by a woman like Chasity-let alone marry her. This woman was as ghetto as ghetto gets. I tried to rationalize our situation and overlook her ignorance. But I found it to be impossible; she would always tell Marcus "*You better not have my child around that bitch.*" Little did she know, he did the exact opposite of her demands, and besides she might as well have gotten use to me because I would soon become Mrs. Marcus Antwon Barnes. Marcus and I had recently gotten engaged.

I had no idea who was speeding down our driveway in a black Mustang GT with tinted windows once I'd made it back home after my altercation with Terrence. I could tell from the way the car was being driven that it was not about to be a pleasant visit.

"Didn't I tell you I don't want my child around that bitch?" Chasity asked Marcus stepping out of the car. "Come over here Lil Mark" She yelled furiously.

Marcus Jr. was helping me get the groceries out of the car.

Chasity was about five feet tall 125 pounds, dark skinned, with a short haircut, and a mouth full of gold. She was straight hood.

"Chat don't come around here starting no shit, I don't have time for it today!" Marcus Sr. argued.

"Oh you ain't got time for it" She said punching Marcus.

"Chat stop hitting me now"

She was attacking him really bad in front of their son. He was no longer helping with groceries, instead he was crying. Quickly, I took the groceries into the house. Angel was in the car asleep. So I hurriedly went back outside to my vehicle. I took Angel into the house and put her down for a nap. Next I went back outside to get Lil Marcus so that I could calm him down. That's when Chasity and I got into an argument.

"Bitch, this ain't got nothin' to do with you!" Chasity snapped at me.

"I know it doesn't, the only thing that I'm trying to do is get Lil Marcus."

"Bitch don't put your hands on my child because if you do I'm gon' fuck you up"

"You gon' fuck who up? Not me. And I'm not going to be too many more of your bitches" I snapped at her.

"Calm down baby" Marcus told me.

"You calling that bitch your baby in front of me" Chasity asked as if she was jealous.

"Yeh, I'm his baby soon to be wife" I told her waving my engagement ring in her face.

"Marcus you better get your bitch, before she is finger-less."

"Alexis baby go take Lil Marcus in the house, so that I can talk to Chasity"

"Don't touch my fucking child" She grabbed Marcus Jr. by the arms. "Go and get in the damn car"

"Don't pull on him like that. Are you fucking crazy" Marcus yelled.

"Don't tell me how to handle my son and you might as well be ready to pay child support, I'm gon' make sure you don't have a dime to spend on that bitch."

"I'll make it easier for you I'll take child support out on myself" Marcus told her.

Marcus didn't have a mean bone in his body. Not one time did he disrespect Chasity, even though really and truly she deserved it. That was the first time that I met Chasity and I knew on that very day, she was going to be another obstacle I would have to overcome.

32

ALEXIS

"Tell me its mines." Marcus insisted as he pumped inside of me. My legs were getting weak from having numerous orgasms. His muscled arms held them tight as he dipped in and out of my vagina as we stood against the wall in our bedroom.

"Tell me its mines" He demanded again.

"It yours" I moaned proudly, my moan echoing because I was about to cum. The way he looked at me while he penetrated back and forth was a weakness for me…him looking at me that way was enough to make me explode.

It was around six thirty a.m. on Christmas day and we were trying to get our rocks off before Angel and Jr. awoke to open their Christmas presents.

"I'm about to cum inside of you" Marcus grunted, before sticking his tongue in my mouth.

"I want you to. I want to have your baby" I informed him.

After about fifteen more minutes of straight banging up our bedroom wall Marcus burst inside of me.

I hopped in the shower afterwards and Marcus hopped in right behind me. We washed each other's bodies and about fifteen minutes later we were done showering. We got dressed and Marcus went downstairs to start breakfast. I went into Jr.'s room and awoke him. Then I went into Angel's room to awake her. I flipped on the light switch.

"Angel wake up baby girl let's go and see what Santa left for you under the tree." I began to shake her. "Angel wake up Baby" She still didn't respond. I felt her pulse it was beating, but very slow. "Oh my God! Angel...can you hear mommy baby?" I shook her harder. "HELLPPP... Marcus." I screamed.

I heard Marcus running up the staircase before he came barging down the hallway "What's wrong baby?" He asked as he entered the room. Lil Marcus stood beside me with a confused expression on his face.

"Call 911 Angel is not responding" I cried out.

He ran out of the room and returned quickly with his cellular attached to his ear "My little girl is not responsive" he told the 911 dispatcher.

"No" I screamed sobbing over Angel's body. "No... No.... No" Tears ran down my cheeks and snot trickled out of my nose. "Do something to save her. Do

196

something" I shouted to Marcus. "Oh God I'm sorry for every bad thing that I have done in my life but please don't take my child away from me" I prayed.

Marcus was still on the phone with the 911 dispatcher as he fell down to the floor to console me.

33

ALEXIS

I sat there alone as I tried to prepare myself for what I knew, the doctor was about to tell me.

"I'm so sorry but we were unable to stabilize Angel. She suffered with an aneurysm to the brain, and she is not breathing on her own. The respirator is breathing for her."

"Noooooooooo!" I screamed loudly as I fell to my knees once again.

Marcus asked the doctor "When can we see her?"

"You can go and see her at any time but there's only two people allowed per visit."

"Baby it's time to visit Angel" Marcus told me. "It's time to say our goodbyes"

"I want to go and see my baby girl and tell her that she can't leave me. It is not her time to go. She is going to bury me I am not going to bury my child. Now she just needs to rest and she is going to wake up."

"Baby I am so sorry that this happened to Angel, but you have to--"

Marcus didn't finish his sentence because I cut him off "Don't you say it...don't you dare give up on her." I walked into the intensive care unit.

She was laying there helpless. I felt as though she was begging for me to help her. I didn't want to accept the fact that I would never hear her sweet little voice say mommy again and I would never hear her laugh or see her beautiful smile again. In my mind my little girl wasn't dead. I lay my head next to her; I wanted to hear that she was going to be okay. I wanted to hear that she was going to wake up and that I would be able to take her home. I held her hand and said to her.

"Hey baby girl. The doctors are saying that there is nothing else that they can do for you but I know that they just don't know what they are talking about. I know that God didn't put you in my life to take you away from me so soon. Oh baby you have so much more life to live. So much more. I'm going to go with you to pick out your prom dress, and then your graduation dress, and your wedding dress. I want to be able to sit up late at night and talk about what boys have a crush on you, when you hit your teenage years. We're going to have mother daughter arguments. And then I'm going to give you motherly advice when you have your first child. You just have to wake up baby." I wiped the tears from my eyes. "I remember when I first held you in my arms you were so tiny but you liked to eat and in no time you were a big and healthy baby. The day I brought you home was the happiest day of my life. I vowed to myself that I would always protect you. I hope that you can hear me baby" I began to cry loudly. "What am I going to do without you? I don't want to live one day without hearing your sweet little voice. So please...baby please. Don't leave me." I begged.

Marcus grabbed me and squeezed me tightly. "Everything is going to be okay...everything is going to be okay"

Three weeks later, Angel was still in the hospital and her health still hadn't turned around. But my daily routine consisted of me getting up and visiting her. This particular morning I was getting dressed so that I could go to the hospital, when my mobile started ringing. I pressed the TALK button.

"Hello" I said slowly because I recognized the number and I knew that it was the hospital.

"Hi Mrs. Johnson, This is doctor Hamilton. The reason for this call is because I've been trying to get in touch with your husband but I can't reach him. I'm not sure what funeral home is supposed to pick up your deceased daughter."

I started to feel dizzy like I always did when I heard devastating news. "What do you mean deceased?" I puzzled.

"Your husband told us to pull the plug on your daughter this morning he said that you'd agreed on it together."

"Terrence and I are not married anymore. Aren't you guys supposed to check with both parents before you do something that serious? We are both supposed to sign the paperwork"

"Well being that your hus—I'm sorry." She cleared her throat. "Doctor Johnson works at this hospital. We thought that he was telling the truth."

"I am going to sue that damn hospital" I screamed before I threw my mobile into the wall furiously.

I walked in circles around the island in the kitchen before I decided to call Terrence. I remained calm when he answered.

"Yeh" He said.

"Hey, where you at? I want to meet you somewhere so that we can talk about what the plans are for Angel."

"I'm at home" He informed me.

After I hung up the phone with Terrence I collected a box of matches from the kitchen drawer. I walked outside and grabbed the gas can that Marcus uses for his motorcycle. "Lucky me" I mumbled amongst myself, because it was filled with petro. I hopped into my car and in no time I was parking my car in front of Terrence's house. I closed my car door quietly as I stepped out of my vehicle, carrying the gas can.

I sprinkled the gas around Terrence's house before I lit the match and tossed it onto the trail of petro. I stood there and watched his house go up in flames.

He always joked that chocolate melts better in your mouth than it does in your hand (a sexual joke). And

201

his black ass sure did melt.

I was as nervous as the day that I lost my virginity as I drove back home. I was popping pill after pill of the Xanax that I had been taking for years. I finally made it home. As soon as I walked through the door I dropped everything to the floor, and ran straight towards the kitchen. I scrambled through the cabinets in search of the bottle of Moscoto that Marcus had opened the day before. I found it and used it to chase down the remainder of the pills. I went into the living room and lay back on the sofa. I wanted to die...I wanted to be with Angel. I wanted to leave my troublesome life.

For the next few hours I went in and out of consciousness and the next thing I knew I was being carried away from my home in a stretcher.

After maybe an hour of getting my stomach pumped in the ambulance truck, I'm now lying in a hospital bed, with an IV attached to my arm.

I can hear everything that Marcus is saying to me. I hear him confessing his love for me. I feel him squeezing my hand, and telling me that I have to pull through.

"Lord I hope that you have my back right now. You've helped me through so many situations. But this is the time that I need you the most. Please don't take away the best thing that ever happened to me. I'm begging you. I'm going to be a mess without her. I need her. I can't live without her she is the air in my lungs, the blood that pumps my heart. She means everything to me, but there is no need for me to tell you how good she is. You already know, you created her. What do you want me to do? I'll be a better person. I'll give my life to you. I will do whatever it takes. Just please I beg you, don't take my better half away from me." Marcus pleads.

"Marcus" I say with a weak voice as I open my eyes.

" Baby you scared me" Marcus says smiling at me.

"I'm sorry" I say weakly.

"Shh… Shh… Shhh. Don't worry about that right now I just want you to concentrate on getting better so that I can take you home." He says to me as he rubs his hand through my hair.

"I'm just so tired Marcus, I'm tired of fighting. I'm tired of all this pain in my life."

"Baby just get some rest and when you get out of here we are going to take a vacation, hell we can even move if you want. We can go where ever you want to go. You just get away for a while"

"I can't--" I start to cough really badly.

"Baby just try and get some rest"

"I can't--" I start to cough again.

I grab Marcus's hand and say. "I can't--"
FLATLINED.

"Baby…no…no…no…nooooooooooo!   Somebody help…somebody help pleasssse!" Marcus screams.

Committed 2 Deception Part 2

Coming soon!!!

www.ingramcontent.com/pod-product-compliance
Lightning Source LLC
Chambersburg PA
CBHW030448250626
47154CB00003BA/1181